Suddenly, a figure stepped out from one of the paintings. First a foot on the rug, then the entire body, and finally a long, dark cape.

In the darkness, Alex could see two red eyes, glimmering.

"It's an illusion, right Alex?" Otis's gargoyle voice was riddled with fear. "Right? Just an illusion—"

"No Otis." Alex watched as a hand moved out of the mist. The fingers unfurled. "It's not."

Otis shook his gargoyle head. "Oh bats are we in trouble."

"Children," the vampire said. One foot moved in front of the other, gently. Alex could see the dark boots on the red carpet. "Come and speak with me. There's nothing to fear."

Which, of course, they all knew was a big fat lie.

Otis groaned.

Angelica screamed.

And the mist swirled up and twisted towards them as the vampire approached.

There was nothing left to do. Now they *had* to go into the room. No matter what was in there, or who . . .

"RUN!" Alex yelled.

VAMPIRE BOY

BY ARIC CUSHING

Grand & Archer

Text Copy © 2014 Aric Cushing
Illustrations © Max Lawson
Text Design © Collin McDowell
Title Font Design © Ray Larabie
Glyph Design © Manfred Klein

Summary: The story of Alex Vambarey, a white haired vampire boy, and his adventures during his first year at the Carpathian Academy. There, with his new gargoyle friend, Otis, and a Druid named Edwald, they try to solve Principal Whitlock's 'challenge' riddle, and win the school prize.

The Library of Congress has catalogued
the paperback edition of this work as follows:
Cushing, Aric — 1st ed.

ISBN 978-1-929730-01-8
ISBN 978-1-929730-04-9
[1. Vampires—Fiction. 2. Magic—Fiction. 3. Fantasy—Fiction.
4. Castles—Fiction. 5. Family—Fiction. 6. Halloween—Fiction.]
7. Horror—Fiction.
I. Title. II. Title: Vampire Boy [Fic]

First Grand & Archer Publishing Edition 2016
Printed in Canada

VAMPIRE BOY

BY ARIC CUSHING

CONTENTS

Contents

CONTENTS

EXCERPT FROM BOOK 2
VAMPIRE VALLEY

DEAR READER

THIS TALE BEGAN WHEN MY MOTHER TOOK ME TO A FAIR
AND PAID AN ARTIST TO DRAW MY PORTRAIT . . .
"DO YOU WANT TO RIDE AN ANIMAL IN THE PICTURE?"
"YES!" I SAID.
"WHAT KIND?"
"SPIDER!"

Me at 6 years old.

COME WITH ME.
TO A WORLD WHERE HALLOWEEN NEVER ENDS,
AND THE STARS ARE HOPEFUL AND BRIGHT.

THE
CARPATHIAN
DICTIONARY

(EXCERPT)

1. **darkday** ~ Equivalent to a human day. Daytime.
2. **darknight** ~ Equivalent to a human night. Nighttime.
3. **trés bien** ~ French phrase meaning very good, or fantastic!
4. **adultwise** ~ Wisdom, or adult knowledge.
5. **Transopolis** ~ The vampire city.
6. **Voivodes** ~ Vampires that are inclined to follow the good.
7. **Darklings** ~ Vampires that are inclined to follow the bad, or evil road.
8. **full moon** ~ A moon that is half as bright as the human sun. A full moon can only be seen during a darkday (human daytime).
9. **crescent moon** ~ A moon that can only be seen at night, or in Carpathia, during a darknight (human nighttime).
10. **druid sense** ~ Intuition, a feeling of knowing what is going to happen.
11. **Oh Creepers!** ~ Means Oh shoot! or Jeepers! or shucks!
12. **tut tut tut (a gargoyle expression)** ~ Means cool, or the best, or excellent!
13. **heyduke** ~ A village elder, or councilman.
14. **bonjour** ~ The French word for 'greetings' or 'good day'.

1

BABY

"*His* hair is white," Nurse Bella proclaimed, "just like the prophecy."

Cassandra Vambarey sat upright in her hospital bed. She stared down at her newborn boy and smiled. "Yes, Alex of the white hair and blue eyes."

"It is definitely *white*," Nurse Bella insisted. Her tone was all snippy.

The boy had pale skin too, like any baby vampire, and tiny pointed teeth. Not to mention little wiggly fingers.

Nurse Bella's foul temperament, strangely enough, was not because of the baby's odd white hair, but solely because of the hospital decor. Recently it had been remodeled by some young whipper snapper, and now reflected the new 'modern' style. A word she most definitely disliked—*modern*. Luckily the outside of the hospital still looked like a castle. Imagine, vampires without stone walls, or cobwebs, or coffins? Did the young upstart plan on changing those as well? And what about the cobweb maker? Had that gone out of style too? Were they now going to start removing all the cobwebs from the hospital?

Nurse Bella looked down to Cassandra and the boy Alex. At least she would never have to worry about them. Cassandra was of the old ways, and still had a home that looked like a good old fashioned tomb.

Cassandra took her eyes away from Alex and looked up. It was time. "If the door is smashed in," she said, "you know what to do."

Bella's mind blew apart. "What! No, no, no, no. Everything will be fine. Everything will be just fine!"

"Nonetheless, the passage is behind me." She grabbed Nurse Bella's arm. "Do not hesitate. If you do, everything will be lost."

Nurse Bella threw her hands in the air. She couldn't see it, but her nurse cap was all a-muddle.

"If anything happens, take him from my arms," Cassandra demanded. Her eyes were on fire. "And rush him into the passage. Do not wait on me. Not even for a moment."

"The passage," Nurse Bela repeated. She glanced over her shoulder to the wall-length tapestry that hid the escape route. "I will. He will be safe. No matter what."

"Good," Cassandra said, satisfied, and turned to her child. She kissed him on the forehead for luck. "My boy. My darling boy. If I never see you again . . . I want you to know that you are *loved*. You are the most loved child in the whole world." Cassandra's hair fell down around him like a protective shield. "And no matter what may lay ahead—no matter what comes your way . . . I promise you—my love will be your magic."

"Is that him?" It was Barnabus who asked, Hillock Green's constable.

"Yes," replied John Vambarey, who stood with the other heydukes (leaders of the Hillock Green township) at the top of Hospital Hill. This was Alex's father. A tall, proud man, with salt and pepper hair, black rimmed glasses, and a strong, prominent nose.

A towering vampire walked towards them. The face was shrouded by a hooded cloak and the cape's train slithered at the rear.

"The grass is burning behim him," someone said.

Which was true. In the vampire's wake, the grass curled and blackened like the burning of a scarecrow's straw.

Barnabus's eyebrows shot up as his hands flew out from his sides. This normally jolly man was now fear-ridden, and the result was a face that looked very much like a blowfish. "Is he going to kill us?"

John nodded. "I don't know. But if he tries, he will have a hard time of it."

And he was right. For behind them stood the entire township of Hillock Green. Every man, woman, and vampire child: their faces proud against the backdrop of night sky, and their bodies frozen like statues in front of the hospital doors. The war was about to begin, and they were ready.

Craftina, another heyduke, stepped forward. Her bright blue hair fluttered against her orange cape. "John, I don't believe he will take the boy by force."

"I pray you're right."

Her voice wavered. "And if he should try?"

"Then we have no choice but to *destroy* him." John looked at her. "Our world depends on it."

All the heydukes turned to each other, and nodded, for they knew the gravity of which John spoke.

The vampire in the black cloak reached them.

Everything seemed to stop.

The vampire's name was Deleter, and though evil, bowed before the townspeople he was about to kill.

John returned the bow, (for this was the vampire way, even amongst heroes and villains) and repositioned himself with his arms crossed.

"Where is the child?" Deleter asked, slowly

John answered, "Safe. And away from you."

The heydukes sucked in their breath.

Deleter's face was hidden, but his reply was nice and sarcastic. "Really? And you believe *you* are powerful enough to stop me?"

Barnabus covered his mouth with his hand. The terror had welled up in his stomach.

"No Deleter. But maybe all of us can."

The pair of narrow eyes beneath the hood seemed to take in the vampires on the hill. "Perhaps," was the vampire's answer. The word came out slow. Way too slow. Like maybe he knew something—something they didn't.

John breathed out and said, "So I am asking you to *please* leave."

The answer was silence.

The vampire Deleter reached up and carefully pulled back his hood.

As soon as Deleter's face was revealed, a woman, nervous Noretta, screamed.

The other villagers, all of whom seemed so strong before, were immediately petrified with fear. Some of them gasped, one of them fell to his knees, and a young girl—Clara Heart—fainted dead away.

John stepped back, his face a painting of shock.

"Well John. What do you think?" Deleter asked, with a smile. "Am I disqualified from the beauty contest?"

No one could take their eyes off the strange creature that now stood before them. The skin was cracked and broken, and from the sides of the head, two black horns projected up from the skull. This wasn't a vampire. It was a devil. With glowing green eyes and faded yellow skin. Not a pretty sight let me tell you. And certainly not a vampire you would invite to dinner!

"Deleter. What have you *done*?"

"Exactly what you never did John. Advanced. From vampire to devil. *Ascended*."

5

"Actually, from the looks of you, I would say you have *descended*."

Deleter snarled. "Bring me the child and you can keep your pathetic lives."

John knew if he backed down now, they were lost. "I prefer to keep my pathetic life, *and* the child thank you. Now we ask you again—leave this place."

"Or what?" Deleter asked. He waited for a reply. When none was forthcoming, he tipped his head back and laughed. His shark-teeth glimmered in the moonlight. "I haven't laughed in a long, long time."

"From the looks of you, I didn't think you could laugh at all," John said, with great pluck.

Deleter, enraged, pointed to John. "Bring him to me!"

"No," John said, simply, "I won't."

The villagers tensed up, in unison.

This was it. The moment they had been dreading.

"I see," Deleter said, sighing. He let his hands fall to his sides. "Pity." He turned to the town below. "Behold," he said, with much sweetness, "the end of your miserable Hillock Green, *and* your simpleton tombs."

With that, everyone watched as a wave of black bats swept into the town from nowhere. Like a thick black cloud, they flew through the buildings and dropped fireballs onto the helpless structures below.

Barnabus cried out.

Craftina threw her hands up to her face.

And Deleter, with the tone of a king, asked, "Now will you bring him to me?"

6

The wind whistled through the night air, but no one moved.

What would he do with the child? Kill him? Is that what this monster wanted?

All of a sudden, a large cloud of blue smoke—and a whole lot of blue sparkles—exploded in the air between Deleter and the heydukes.

Everyone jerked.

The explosion was immediate, intimidating, and quite colorful.

Professor David Whitlock, the magus of the Carpathian Academy, stepped out of the vapors, and into the tall grass below. He brushed off his cape calmly, and looked up. "I hate it when that happens," he said, for he was clearly covered in glitter, "I *never* get that spell right."

This vampire, who was a Magus of royal lineage, was strikingly handsome. But strange too. His hair was completely white except for a large streak of black running down the middle, and, like the vampire Deleter, exceptionally tall.

Around him, like the puff of a dandelion, the multicolored sparkles floated through the air.

Deleter was startled at first, but composed himself quickly. "David. How nice of you to attend."

Whitlock took a sparkle off the tip of his tongue and flicked it into the air.

"After all," Deleter continued, "you have so many young minds to influence, and direct."

Whitlock raised an eyebrow. "You can drop the sarcasm Deleter."

Deleter pouted, and pushed out his lips like a baby. (Which was very strange, for you seldom see a devil pout.) "*Ohhh David*," he cooed, "you're such a party pooper. You simply get no fun out of life."

Whitlock smiled. "Perhaps. But you and I have a *very* different idea of fun, don't we?"

"Without question," Deleter flared, "but I never said I wanted to *take* the child, did I? I am . . . simply here to pay my respects. A friendly visit, you might say."

"A friendly visit?"

"Yes."

"Oh. How kind of you. How very, very thoughtful. A friendly visit to burn down the boy's home. And his village."

"David!" Deleter threw his hand to his chest as if deeply offended. "You make it sound so . . . *diabolical*."

Whitlock's face hardened as he turned to the village below. The bouncing fireballs had already annihilated the town park. With one thrust, he threw his hand into the air and heralded a spell with one word: "Torrentia!"

The heydukes watched (with much relief) as thick clouds—from nowhere—unfolded in the sky and dropped water onto the flaming streets below.

Whitlock returned his gaze to Deleter. "I think the town of Hillock Green is in no need of your 'friendly visits'. Let's say . . . they're a bit too hot to handle."

Deleter replied, easily, "Well, you of all people know how I love to play with fire."

Whitlock's eyes flashed with vengeance. "Yes. And now that I see you—face to face—you've clearly been playing with too much of it."

Deleter ignored the dig. "I deserve to know the child's name."

Whitlock answered sharply, "You deserve," and he punctuated the last word with great venom, "*nothing*."

The devil became playful again, and shrugged. "Well . . . maybe not."

"Now," Whitlock said, with finality, "I bid you good-night. A boy has been born, and a celebration is in order. A festivity in which you are *not* invited."

At this, Deleter turned away from Whitlock and fixed his gaze on John. "Goodbye John Vambarey." He paused. "Since I could not kill you tonight, I've left you a gift instead. Why don't you share it with all your towns-folk buffoons."

Barnabus stepped forward. "What gift?" His eyes fluttered from terror.

"I do not know Barnabus," Whitlock replied. He pushed his large white lock of hair, which had become displaced, back to the top of his head. "But the boy is safe."

Deleter smiled and replaced his hood. "Farewell Hillock Green. Until we meet again."

Slowly, the devil vampire turned, and moved back down the burnt trail of grass.

"Where is he going?" someone asked, fearfully.

As if answering the question, a wooden staircase ma-

terialized out of thin air, and shot up to the sky from the path. At the end, a red door floated in suspension.

The villagers watched as Deleter ascended the steps. When the monster reached the top, he opened the door with a wave of his hand. No one knew where the door went, but when opened, you could see a rectangle of blackness beyond. Like a sky with no stars.

Barnabus was helping poor Clara Heart up from the ground. She had finally regained consciousness.

Deleter glanced over his shoulder. He gave all the villagers a nice, cute little wave as if to say, *I'll be back, don't worry*, and then stepped into the darkness, and disappeared.

The door shut with a *whack*.

Whitlock turned to the townspeople and stared into their frightened, eager eyes. He knew what they were thinking.

The portal had not disappeared, but had remained in the air, hovering. If it was a passage to Hillock Green, what would prevent the monster from using it again?

David Whitlock turned to the villagers. "Hear me!" His voice was clear and deep. "Vampires of the Green. We must work in alliance. We must work together and with one mind."

In the distance, the main doors of the hospital shot open.

Cassandra Vambarey emerged, somewhat triumphantly, with Alex cradled in her arms. She moved through the grass as Nurse Bella followed her.

"Cassandra!" John yelled. It was a forceful demand to return to the safety of the hospital.

"John," Whitlock whispered. He put a hand on the man's shoulder. "We need the boy."

Though Cassandra had heard her husband, she did not stop until she had reached them.

"Magus Whitlock," she said, proudly, "Alex will put up the first seal."

Barnabus was peering around, quite confused, as were all the heydukes. Even Craftina.

"Thank you my dear." And with that, Magus Whitlock raised his hands in the air. "Hear me Hillock Green! Let not the course of this evil bring forth evil. Defy the devil! Consider him an enemy to vampirekind. Together we will lock a door on one who has betrayed his brethren." He paused as the villagers looked on. All of their arms had risen into the sky. "This night, a child will lead us!"

With this cue, Cassandra leaned down, gently, and whispered into Alex's wee ear.

Whatever she did say, Alex must have understood it, for he immediately threw up a teensy weensy fist.

The first lock materialized—instantly—hovered in the air, and then slammed itself against the red door with a heavy thud.

John moved to his wife's side and put his arm around her.

"PUT UP YOUR SEALS HILLOCK GREEN!" Whitlock yelled. "For tonight we protect the *good* in our world. And a boy."

Locks began to pop, all of them out of thin air, and slam themselves against the door. *Bang! Zip! Clunk! Clink!* And soon the door was covered. You couldn't even see a peep of the wood. The locks just kept going and going. Lock upon lock upon lock. Locking the locks that were locking other locks that had locked the door hanging in space.

The last lock was done by a girl. A quite small girl, by the way, who was only three years old.

Poppy emerged from the crowd, dressed in a bright pink tutu, and a bejewelled tiara. Her curly red hair bubbled up on her head like cotton candy, and in her right hand she held a wand, of the home-made fashion, and not quite magical.

When she reached Magus Whitlock, she stopped a few feet in front of him, shook the wand, and then gave out a squeal of delight.

The last lock materialized, with a *blip!*, and sat on top of all the others. Mini-sized, incidentally, and colored in bright purple polka-dots.

It was a very strange sight, that was for sure. A staircase leading up to what was once a door, which was now a pile of locks.

But there you have it!

Poppy plopped down on her bottom, satisfied, and started searching the grass for faeries.

"I think that does it," Whitlock said, with finality.

The nervous townsfolk, who were scattered over the

green, waited for his command.

"On the count of three—with all of us together now—Hands in the air! Snap!" He raised his long white fingers into the sky above his head. "One . . . two . . . three . . ."

The villagers held their breath.

"SNAP!"

Everyone *snapped*.

Including little Poppy.

The creepy staircase, locks, *and* the door disappeared in one big *KAAPOOF!*

Applause erupted from the relieved villagers.

Magus Whitlock smiled. He brushed both of his palms together as if to rid them of a pesky dust.

John Vambarey kissed his wife on the forehead and tickled Alex's little nose. The evil was gone. At least for tonight.

Magus Whitlock did not stay much longer. There was far too much to do, and plan for. But before he went, he leaned down and kissed the forehead of the white haired boy.

The star child, he thought to himself. The boy who would one day save them from the sun . . . and themselves.

Alex Vambarey.

Of Hillock Green.

2

THE CONVERSATION

Alex stood in front of his father's chair and stared into the crackling fire. He had grown to a medium height for his age, was thin, and besides his one best friend, kept mostly to himself. "It's a little early to go to school, isn't it?" he asked.

Cassandra looked at him over her knitting spool. Nothing had changed since he had been born. Her beautiful black hair still spilled out over her shoulders, her eyes were still large and round and slanted at the ends, and her high cheekbones still had a couple freckles. "But you are starting early darling."

Alex nodded. "I wonder what kind of kids will be there? Besides vampires I mean."

His mother didn't answer.

Now, just so you know, there are two types of vampires born into Carpathia. The first sort are darklings, which many consider to be evil, and the second batch are the voivodes, which many consider to be good. Naturally, Alex was a voivode.

"Now, to bed," Cassandra said sweetly. She rolled up her ball of yarn. "You'll need as much rest as you can tomorrow."

Alex went to his room, put on his pumpkin pajamas, and crawled into his coffin. How could he even think of sleep when he was supposed to leave tomorrow?

Alex turned his head and peaked over the rim of his coffin. Photographs dotted his bed chamber walls. Why not take them? Maybe he could put them up in his room at school?

Vladimir Whip stared back at him with one hand over his chest and his face raised regally to the sky. While Ekaterina Clump, Prime Minister Extraordinaire, peered, with one eyebrow raised. They certainly didn't look like they wanted to be moved, that was for sure. And what about the photographs of the kooky zoo animals he loved so much? Or the snapshot of his friend, Varney?

Alex resolved himself. "No. I *will* leave. But not until I find out—"

And with a sudden determination, Alex jumped out of his coffin, rushed across the room, and grabbed his cape off its hanger. Tonight he would do it. Yes! Before he left he would solve the mystery that had baffled the villagers of the Green. Tonight he would see what was forbidden and become a hero! He would discover the mystery of the fire forest and return unscathed. He would solve the riddle of how the trees always burned and never went out. What an adventure to tell his new friends at school. And what a feat!

Alex tip-toed to his chamber door, opened it quietly, and peeked down the hall. Besides the crackling logs in the fireplace, and a mouse (vampires have incredible hearing you know), everything was quiet.

He waited, and listened.

Nothing.

His parents had to be asleep. They had to be!

With a quick jump, Alex leapt into the corridor, shot to the end, and almost ran into—his parents! They hadn't gone to sleep at all. Alex realized the only reason they *didn't* notice him was because of their discussion. It went like this.

"When do you want to tell him?"

John Vambarey walked from one side of the fireplace to the other, his shoes clacking against the stone. "I do not know. Something this . . . secret." He paused, "This important . . ."

His mother spoke confidently. "He is young, but not in mind."

"Yes. But boys grow into men very quickly," his father replied.

"Do they?" His mother asked.

"Yes," his father repeated, sternly, "boys grow into men *very* quickly."

"Well, I prefer not to speed up the process," she said.

What in the name of Carpathia does that mean? Alex thought to himself.

Cassandra added, "I don't know. There is no right answer."

Alex heard the swish of his father's cloak. Unlike his mother, his father always wore his cape—"Out of respect for history," he would say—but usually it bothered him, and he always ended up tossing it about. His mother never wore her cape.

His father spoke again. "It's much too dangerous." A long silence followed. "Someone could use it against him. Especially because he is so young."

"But would they?"

"Yes. Maybe even his friends."

"No no, not at his age. I think you're being pessimistic." His mother had picked up her needles. They tinked against each other as she wove.

His father gave a little laugh. "Well. No one would disagree that I am a bit of a pessimist."

"You are *not* a pessimist. Don't say such foolish things."

"But you just said—never mind." Alex heard a goblet clatter against the fireplace's stone mantle. His father had put down his drink. "It is best to be truthful, if nothing else."

Why did adults always have to speak in riddles? Why not just say something outright? In plain vampirish.

Alex could feel himself beginning to squirm. He had always felt that there was something they hadn't told him. Something they were keeping a secret. But he never knew what.

"I'm always truthful with Alex," his father said.

"I know dear."

"But this . . . *must* wait until he's older. I really feel that it must."

What was it!

Alex wiggled. Woops. And then pressed himself harder against the stone wall. If he moved an inch, they would hear him. Even a toe . . .

"Yes. For his own safety we cannot tell him. I am sure we must wait."

"But *when* do we tell him?" his mother asked gently. "When?"

His father breathed out and picked up the goblet on the mantle. "When the time is right, it will present itself." There was a long silence. "But only when the time is right."

3

DREAM OF A HUMAN SON

Varney, Alex's best friend, trudged beside him through the wet grass.

Alex had crawled through Varney's window, shook him awake from a dead trance, and convinced him, as he always did, to sneak out.

"I don't know why I let you drag me into doing all these crazy things. You're always *dragging* me to do these crazy things. And we always get caught. Always! I don't think we've ever NOT been caught. Do you know—."

A word on Varney. He wasn't troubled. He did not have a secret. He was very short. He was easily excited. And—when something interested him, and so many things did—he exploded with energy, and usually waved his arms. The most distinctive characteristic about Varney was his blonde ringlets, which jutted out from the

ARIC CUSHING

top of his head like curley-cues.

Varney looked over to Alex. There was something in his friend's face that looked different. "What's wrong with you? We're going, aren't we? I said I would go, didn't I?"

"It's not that," Alex said.

"It's not?"

"No."

Alex wondered if he should tell his friend about what he had heard. About the secret his parents had been keeping from him.

Varney tried to pat down his locks. The ringlets popped back up on his head like springs. "Did you hear about that boy that disappeared in the fire forest?"

"His name was Vartok," Alex answered.

"Why didn't the elders go and find him?"

Alex responded, absently, "I think they tried. But they couldn't. He just vanished."

Varney nodded. "Vartok. I never saw what he looked like. He lived on the other side of the cemetery. You know he was a *darkling*."

Both boys climbed up and over a small hill, then stopped.

Ahead, two ancient statues rose up from the ground, their stone faces covered in weeds. To walk between them meant to leave the township of Hillock Green, not to mention the safe spells that protected the village.

"I've never been this far," Alex said.

"Neither have I." Varney shivered and glanced over

to Alex. "Why are we doing this again?"

The grass rustled as the trees rose up like strange omens of doom. This was the portal that led you into the further reaches of Carpathia, and beyond.

A twig snapped in the distance.

"Did you hear that?" Varney asked, his voice jittery. "Maybe we should go back."

An owl hooted.

Alex was about to respond, but there was no time. An explosion of light detonated in front of the statues. Smoke zipped out from nowhere.

Varney yelled, "What is it!"

Before they knew what was happening, two figures materialized in front of them.

Alex tried to wave the smoke away, but it was much too persistent for that. It pointed at him, very deliberately, in the shape of a huge finger.

"I think we're in trouble," Varney mumbled. His face had turned the color of a bright red tomato.

"You most certainly are," retorted Bundica Ruff. She stood with her canary yellow cape draped over her body, eyebrows raised, and face ready for battle. Alex's mother stood behind her. "Wellllllllll?" Bundica insisted.

Varney shrugged. "Sorry mom."

"That is not an appropriate response," she clucked, and grabbed him by an ear. "You don't know *what* could be creeping out here. Vampire killers! And who knows what else."

Cassandra glided to Alex and put her hand on his

shoulder. Calmly, she kneeled down and looked into his eyes. "Darling, you were so loud sneaking out, it was impossible *not* to hear you. We must work on that."

And the two mothers took them home and tucked them into their coffins.

"I've been having nightmares," Alex said.

Cassandra pushed the blanket up to his chin. She had made it when he was born. A weaved quilt of blue-green leaves. "What kind of nightmares?"

"I wake up and I am human. I see a human sun. It is a large circle that is on fire and it burns me and then I die."

"There is no such sun in our world," his mother answered. She brushed a strand of hair away from his forehead. "And to be human. I'm not sure what I can say to that. Their lives are—"

"What mother. What are they?" All these years he had wondered.

She considered it. "Difficult. But in a different way than ours. You see, they must die. *But*, in this death-coming, they have immeasurable gifts. You possess some of those. I do. Everyone in Carpathia does."

"Really?"

"The humans are our fathers and mothers. We are their *descendents*."

Alex sat up a little. He rested his arm on his pillow. "But we die too."

"Yes, but it is a choice."

"Have you ever met one? A human I mean."

She became serious. "Yes. I have."

"I want to meet one," Alex said.

His mother smiled. "Maybe you will. You never know."

Alex wanted to ask her what the secret was. What had they been hiding from him all these years? But somehow he couldn't. "Sometimes I feel so old and so young at the same time. I know that sounds really weird."

His mother nodded. "Sweetlove . . . *I understand*. It is a strange feeling that never quite goes away."

Alex thought about this, and then looked up and into her eyes. "It makes me restless mother. Sometimes I can't sleep."

Cassandra touched his hand. "I know. That is why your father paces . . . in front of the fire."

After his mother was gone, Alex stared at the stone of his bed chamber's ceiling. The crickets were chirping outside and a wolf was howling from some distant hill.

"Ah, the children of the night! What sounds they make!"

Who had said that anyway? Varney's dad? He couldn't remember.

Alex tossed in his coffin as the worriesome questions tumbled through his mind. Maybe he would have strange creatures for classmates? That could happen.

Or maybe he would just hate all of it and want to come home?

There's no point thinking about it! What's the point of worrying when you don't even know what's going to happen?!

Which was true of course, but the logic wasn't doing any good. His feelings were there, and they were leading him. Always leading him. Into yearnings for the future, and peculiar grown-up dreams.

What would his father say?

Ha!

He could answer that one pretty easily.

Subject yourself to reason my son. Reason.

And what would his mother say?

The heart is wiser than the head.

Bats! A kid could go crazy from all the wacky, parental advice!

Tomorrow he would leave. Yes. Because reason dictated it (there you go dad!) and his heart wanted it (there you go mom!), and he would see the world. The Carpathian World anyway. And hopefully there *would* be a lot of heart in it, and a lot of reason too.

4

A TUNNEL OF LEAVES

Now is a good time to tell you about the vampire hamlet of Hillock Green. It is very much like your own home town, with a post office, and a grocery store, and little shops that line the street. But here, instead of houses, there are tombs. One after the other as far as the eye can see. With vines on some, midnight flowers on others, and little yards with metal mailboxes. Plus, a grocery store filled with all sorts of delectable vampire foods. Oh yes, and the most lovely vampire park, with slides and grass and odd drooping trees.

Elsa's carriage pulled past all these sights, and stopped in front of the Vambarey tomb at a quarter past twelve. Alex had never seen the woman before, nor her gargantuan black horses.

John spoke first, while Elsa attached the reins to a hook pole. "Good evening Elsa."

"Mr. Vambarey, it has happened at last," she singsonged. Her tone was all fuzzy and warm. "Oh, they must go. They must go." Alex noticed her kinky red hair was like a clown's wig, and her body took up the entire top seat of the carriage.

His father was smiling.

"But ooooohhhh you will have fun my child." She did not get down from her seat, but winked at Alex from atop the brougham. "Do you want to ride on the horses? As you can see, they're quite friendly."

Alex looked at them. Drool dripped from their sharp teeth and their eyes burned like red lanterns in the night. Friendly! They looked like they were about to eat you whole. "Thanks, but I think . . . I'll ride inside."

"Oh the babies will be sad," Elsa hooted, to which one of the horses gave a tiny whinny.

Alex's mother, who stood on the tomb doorstep, leaned down and hugged him. "Goodbye my darling. Write to us of your adventures."

"I will," Alex said.

Cassandra watched as her husband and son traversed the garden path. It was a beautiful night for a journey, and the jasmine was in full bloom.

John opened the lych gate for his son, and both of them took the remaining few steps to Elsa's horse-driven taxi.

"All right, up we go." His father lifted him up and through the buggy's doors.

Alex plopped onto the leather seats and watched as his father climbed in.

Outside, Cassandra was beginning to cry.

The buggy did not move, as expected, but just sat there instead.

John poked his head out the window. "Elsa? Anything wrong?"

Alex could hear her reprimanding Frill and Fran, the two horses. "You both just ate one hour ago for vampire's sake! Now off with you, or no dinner." She twisted her head and peered down. "Don't you worry about a thing Mr. Vambarey. These shires always think they know what's best. When to eat, when to sleep, and when to talk back!"

John laughed and settled back into the buggy. He moved his cape off one shoulder as the wheels began to roll.

Suddenly, Alex jumped up and stuck his head out the window. "I love you mom!" he yelled.

His mother waved to him from their tombstep. "I love you too darling! Dance for me!"

But before he could answer, his father yanked him back inside, and the buggy blasted off.

"Why do they call it a whining tree?" Alex asked.

"Unfortunately, you are about to find out."

This was the first time Alex had ever been beyond the

gates of Hillock Green. As he watched, there were many wonders—clouds shifting overhead, catcalls of wood monsters, and dancing will-o'-the-wisps in the trees.

"Is that the fire forest over there?" Alex asked. He could see the orange-red light burning against the night sky.

"Yes," his father said. "Don't ever try to go there by yourself again."

The carriage turned and moved into a tight spot. The only view now seemed to be the hedges. They pressed in through the windows.

"Did you hear me?"

"Yeah. Sorry."

"Don't apologize. Just don't go there."

Once they were past the forest, Alex felt relieved. There was something in the woods—the trees—that made you feel uneasy. Something . . .

"What is this place?" Alex asked.

The carriage had reached a moat. A small draw-bridge hung lop-sided over the water, and on the other side, there was a THING—for that's all that you could call it—in the middle of the little island.

"Protection for the whining tree."

Alex stuck his head out the window and peered past the bridge. It didn't seem like a tree at all, that was for sure. There was no trunk.

"Here we go," his father said.

The carriage came to an abrupt stop as Elsa's horses neighed, and shook their noses.

Alex could see they were in a clearing, and about twenty feet away there was a massive pile of leaves. Only there was no way to see to the top, no matter how much you tried. The mound went right into the clouds!

John looked down and ruffled his son's hair. "Be strong with that old tree. Don't let him push you around."

Alex looked up to his father, wide-eyed. "What does *that* mean?"

"You'll see."

Elsa opened the carriage door with the end of her whip, and both of them got out.

"Thank you Elsa," John said, and gave her a handsome wink.

Elsa blushed and rolled her eyes. "Anything for your Mr. Vambarey. Don't forget his suitcase."

"I have it." John took Alex's hand and snatched up the valise with his other. Elsa waited by the carriage as John led Alex to the leaves.

As they walked to the humongous heap, Alex wondered if giants were the culprit. Maybe the giants had pushed all the leaves into a pile, and had forgotten to throw them in the garbage.

"All you have to do is touch them," his father said. "Reach your hand out."

Alex did.

As his hand moved towards the closest perky frond, all of them shifted, reallocated, and then parted.

Alex jumped at first, but then started to grin. "Wow. Good trick."

His father laughed. "Yes it is."

They walked through the opening and into the newly created tunnel. The sound of leaves rustled around them like voices from the wind.

John stopped.

A thought flickered into Alex's mind. "Dad. I think I need a bigger cape. I'm growing out of this one."

John's face shifted. Alex noticed the change instantly. "We'll get you a new cape. Don't worry about that. But first I want you to listen."

Alex nodded, but said nothing.

"This is very important. While you're at school, I want you to learn as much as you can. Not just from your classes, but from all the students. Do you understand?"

"Dad, this sounds like a pep talk."

"Yes. Well . . ." he laughed, "I guess it is."

This he could handle. Alex shifted, moved his cape over his shoulders, and settled. "All right, I'm ready. Go ahead."

John chuckled at his son's preparation. "What I really want you to do . . . is learn. Learn from the other kids. Study them."

"All right," Alex replied, but he really didn't know what his father meant, or why it was so important.

"What I mean to say is that some children only make friends with their own kind. This isn't good. Make friends with everyone. Learn from everyone. Soon you'll be a big vampire. And when that happens, when you become adultwise . . . you'll need all the friends you can get."

"I'm good at making friends."

"You are when you try," his father said, "but this past year you . . . haven't been cultivating those friendships."

Alex's face clouded over.

"I'm probably making this more complicated than it is. All you have to do is make friends. That's all I'm saying."

"What if I can't?"

His father looked at him. "Have you been worrying about that?"

Alex shifted from one foot to the other. "Kinda."

"Well don't. Have fun and be your own vampire. Once you do that, your friends will find *you*."

Alex hoped he was right.

They continued on for a bit, and soon stopped at the end of the tunnel. It, too, was made of leaves.

John smiled. "Are you ready?"

Alex nodded. "Yes . . . No! Wait." He paused, then said, "I need to know something."

"Sure. Shoot."

"Dad. What is the secret that . . . thing you and mom don't want to tell me?"

His father looked down to him. "You do surprise me sometimes. And *that* is something I will always be proud of."

Alex smiled.

"I didn't hear you in the hall last night—listening. Ahh, my little creeper." His father always used little

31

creeper as a pet name.

Alex felt a flush of embarrassment. He pressed on anyway. "Dad, I can't go to school all year and not know. It'll drive me crazy."

"It will?"

"Totally."

"All right, but the secret is one you already know." His father paused, "Which, I guess doesn't make it much of a secret."

"How can I know it already?"

"You're a white haired vampire. That's the secret."

Alex's face fell. "That's it? The big secret is I have white hair?"

"Pretty much," his dad sighed. "The ancients say that 'the white-haired ones' are important. Why exactly, no one knows." His father kneeled down and gripped his shoulders. "And you know how your mother worries about you. She doesn't want you to grow up too fast." His father paused. "*But*, there is always a silver lining!"

"There is?"

"Sure! At least it's a secret you won't have to keep."

Alex didn't understand. "Why not?"

"Because everyone knows about it!" John stood up and brushed his son's hair back. "It's the first thing someone sees. Your hair. Now, it is *time* for you to face that good for nothing tree, and tell it a thing or two. All right? And who knows, you might get lucky."

"Lucky?"

"Sure. He might be in a good mood!"

5

SOMETIMES YOU MUST GO ALONE

The door opened onto a vast field, and in the middle, the whining tree's trunk was rooted. As thick as a skyscraper and as withered as a witch's face.

"We have to wait our turn," John said. He led Alex to a small area of happy mushrooms and wildwood. His father pointed to a clearing. "Do you see that patch of grass?"

"By the tree?"

"Yes." John kneeled to his son's height. "Now watch."

In the distance, a large boy stepped forward with a suitcase in one hand and a hat in the other.

Alex watched as the tree twisted. A face was set in the bark, halfway up the trunk. "Name?"

When the tree spoke, all the leaves shuddered.

"Batcakes," the boy squeaked.

Which was not really his name. His actual name was Bradley Greenblack, but no one ever called him Bradley. The nickname had been adopted, even by him, and now no one knew him by anything else.

"What are you here for?" The tree asked sourly.

Batcakes mumbled, "To go in?"

"Well, I suppose that is what everyone is here for. To go in! Everyone always wants to go in! Of course, I forget the darkday each year. BUT, here we are again. Year after year after year. I tell you, by the time this darkday comes, I'm pooped!" The tree leaned back. "What do you think about that?"

"Then how would we get to school?"

"What do I care!"

Suddenly a root burst forth—from the ground—and spit dirt into Batcake's face. It pounded, this swollen thing, like a tapping foot on the floor.

"WELL?" the tree demanded.

Batcakes stared up, terrified.

The tree continued: "Now that I think about it, what *would* happen if I wasn't here? I suppose everyone would find another tree. There's always another tree, isn't there?!"

The voice had become soooo loud even the shrubs were shirking away.

"I don't think there is. I don't know of another tree," Batcakes offered, sheepishly.

"Well there is!" the tree barked. "There are plenty of other trees. Plenty. For goodness sake. Some darkday I will be too old for this. Look at my roots! Old and tired. Oh, but I wish. . . " The eyes in the trunk looked up and into the branches. "You know, I could have been a wily tree on the edge of a cliff, with a view of the great rivers. That could have been me—"

"Dad?" Alex asked.

John looked at his son.

"How long does he go on like this?"

"The first in line always gets it the worst. After that, he just eyes you up and down and opens the door."

"All right! Go ahead," the tree blurted.

A little door in the base of the humongous trunk cracked opened.

Batcakes ran to the door as if his life depended on it.

"Next!" the tree roared.

Alex picked up his suitcase. "Dad. I'm going to go next."

"Sure kiddo. Your mother and I will see you at Halloween." John knelt down again and tapped Alex's nose with his forefinger. "I love ya kid. Go bite 'em dead."

"I will! Thanks dad."

"WHO'S NEXT! For moon's sake, we haven't got all darkday!"

Alex ran to the clearing and stopped.

"What have we here?"

"Alex Vambarey of Hillock Green," Alex answered, firmly. Maybe if he took a strong stance, the tree wouldn't be so grumpy. It was a good idea anyway.

"That's not what I meant," the tree snipped back.

35

Alex froze. "Excuse me?"

The tree rolled it's eyes in total and utter annoyance.

Alex didn't know what to do. He looked back to his father.

John held up a fist as if to say, *be strong, don't let him push you around!*

Alex nodded.

Suddenly the gargantuan tree twisted, the face swept in, and the large wooden nose pointed right between his eyes. "What aaaaarre you?" the tree charged.

"A vampire," Alex replied, and he tried to stand a little straighter.

"You look like a brownie."

"Well I'm not. I'm a vampire."

"Well you look like a brownie."

"You just said that," Alex retorted. This whole thing was beginning to feel like *Alice in Vampireland*. In a minute he was going to fall down a hole with Bunnicula and start talking to the Hatter.

"You're sassy like a brownie," the tree suggested.

Alex didn't know what sassy meant. "I am?"

"Yes."

"Sorry."

"Ahhhh," and the tree gave a hint of a smile. As much as the whining tree could smile, "but maybe humble too."

Alex stood quietly. Maybe if he was just *silent*, the tree would open the door.

"Well . . . do you want to go in or not?"

"Ugh . . . yes. I do."

"Of course you do! Everyone does."

Alex nodded.

"What's the magic word then?"

Was this a trick question?

Alex smiled and said, confidently, "Please."

"NO! That is NOT the magic word. It's pumpkin pie."

"But that's two words."

There was a long pause.

"It is?"

"Yes. Pumpkin. Pie. Two words."

"I thought it was hyphenated," the tree huffed, with a very uppity tone. "Anyway, I'm right. You're wrong. Now what else do you want?"

Alex thought fast. "I just want to get it right next time. The password I mean."

"Oh, I see." The tree leaned back, with its face bending in thought. "Well . . . pumpkin is good. We'll go with that."

"Pumpkin," Alex confirmed.

"And tell all your friends too. If I forget I won't be able to let anyone in. And then they'll all come to *you* for the password. Imagine that! Everyone in the world coming to you? Just to find out a word. You wouldn't last a day under that irritation, let me tell you. Not a day."

"Pumpkin. I won't forget."

"All right. Go on," and the little door at the base of the tree flew open.

Access granted.

37

Alex snatched up his suitcase and ran for it.

He reached the door lickety split, and stopped once inside.

Alex turned and waved at his father triumphantly.

As if sensing this was a sweet goodbye, the tree laughed, viciously, and slammed the door right in his face.

6

A Spiral Staircase

To

Who Knows Where

Alex tried to probe the darkness, but all he could see was the first few steps of a very vague staircase, which seemed to move downward.

"Well, what did you expect?"

Alex looked around. "Who's there?"

"What do you mean, who's there? We're smack dab in the middle of a conversation. This just goes to show you that no one listens anymore! Now get a move on. Down. Go!"

"I can't see anything." Alex shifted his suitcase from one hand to the other.

"*All* vampires can see in the dark," the tree retorted, "even I know that."

Alex wasn't old enough to have acquired his vampire

vision, but he certainly wasn't going to tell the tree that. "Well . . . could you pleeeaasssee turn on the lights?"

There was no verbal response to the question, but small balls of green light popped on and began to glow. They hung in the air like lamp posts, and illuminated a curving staircase. The steps twisted to the left and seemed to go straight down.

"There. Happy?"

"Thanks," Alex said, but he was really thinking to himself, *there is simply no talking to this crazy tree!*

From the light of the suspended spheres, Alex noticed a multitude of faces, buried in the walls on either side of the staircase. Well, not *different* faces that is, but the same one, over and over and over.

Alex took a few steps and inspected one of the profiles. Yes, the face on the inside of the tree was exactly the same as the one on the outside. Same nose.

The eyes shot open.

Alex jerked back.

"20 and 10. 20 and 10. How many children will come through again?"

This was exasperating!

"That's right, keep going," one of them barked, but the others were starting to pick up the chant as well. "Who will affect the world again!"

Alex shook his head, gripped his suitcase tighter, and continued down.

It turned out to be a long descent, and curiously, the staircase seemed to be shrinking with each turn. The walls much more . . . narrow . . . and . . . snug.

"Mr. Tree, excuse me, but—"

Tighter.

"20 and 10, 20 and 10, who will affect the world again!"

Narrower.

Alex could feel his arms rubbing against the stump wall interior.

"Keep going, keep going," one of the faces snapped, while the others continued to chant.

But you couldn't go any further. The passage had become far too compact.

Alex was stuck.

"I can't. There's not enough room."

The nearest face rolled its huge eyes. "Well, why don't you turn sideways. Haven't you thought of that?"

Actually, Alex had not thought of that. He followed the tree's direction, turned sideways, and wiggled another few feet.

Suddenly, he found himself peering right into the eyes of one of the faces. "Hello," it said, quite cheerfully.

Alex looked into the crinkled, carved expression. "Hi," he replied.

"Are you stuck?"

Alex tried to wiggle some more, but gave up. There was just no more wiggle left!

"It looks like you're stuck," the face in front of him said. "The door is right over there though."

Alex turned and looked over his shoulder. Yes, there

was a door there. That was for sure. But what good was it if you couldn't get to it?

"Try popping," the face said.

Alex had no idea what this meant. "Popping?"

"Sure. Squeeze yourself thin, then pop yourself out!"

Alex figured he might as well try it, even though it didn't make any sense at all. There was no such thing as popping. If you could pop yourself out of a situation, surely everyone would be doing it.

But there was no harm in trying. Alex took a deep breathe, focused, shimmied, and—

"Now pop!"

Whether the walls moved outward, or Alex had *actually* gotten thinner, he never knew. But he did fall forward—after the popping—and landed on his bottom. "Ouch."

"All you have to do is pop," one of the faces chirped, very much pleased with itself. "Popping always works."

"Is it always this long to get down the steps?" Alex asked. He pulled himself up and brushed off his cape. There were wood chips all over it.

"Oh no," the tree said.

"Why not?"

"Sometimes it takes a few steps, sometimes a lot of steps. All depends."

"Depends on what?"

"Why, whoever is going through of course."

"That doesn't make sense," Alex articulated, with much irritation. He tried to think of a more direct question. "So why were there so many stairs for *me* then?"

"Very clever, aren't you? Well, I *thought* that we might have some stimulating conversation. But clearly I was wrong!"

The door at the bottom of the staircase boomed open.

Alex didn't know what to say. Suddenly, he thought of something. Turning, he focused on the closest countenance. "Well, maybe next time."

That did it!

All the mouths responded, in accordance: "Well good. That sounds very good. We will have a very good conversation next time." And then they smiled, which was strange, for they were sooo very sour before, and sing-songed, "Good luck!"

"Thank you. But I don't believe in luck."

The tree was surprised. "You don't?"

"No," Alex countered, "I don't."

The tree was quick to answer. "If you do not believe in luck, Alex Vambarey of Hillock Green, you will do very well. Very well indeed."

And a blast of air hit him in the rumpus, and ejected him through the door.

7

THE SEA OF GIANTS

Alex landed on a pile of hay. When he looked back, the tree was gone. Instead, there was a long line of doors, one after the other, opening out from the side of a mountain. Alex knew what they were. Portal doors that took you from one place to another.

"This way," a voice directed.

Alex turned.

A few feet away a wood bridge led to a small wharf. There, a boat sat. A bearded man waved to him from inside the boat.

The man looked like a giant, even though Alex had never really seen one in person. Hair dangled from the boatman's chin to his belly, and his free hand rested on the helm of the vessel. The helm was a gigantic carved dragon.

"What's your name?" the man inquired.

"Alex Vambarey."

"This is your boat. Get in."

Alex examined the wood bridge that led to the small wharf. Beneath it, dark water surged and spouted into the air.

"It's safe," the man yelled to him, "the storm hasn't started."

With that, Alex dashed across the platform, over the wharf, and into the boat. He plopped into the last row and put his suitcase on the floor.

The boat moved up and down, down and up, with every water swell, while the children swayed back and forth like a large pack of disorderly birds. Thunder cracked in the darkness overhead, and the little raft, for it was more of a raft than a boat, threatened to throw them all into the sea—and they hadn't even left the dock!

Alex looked to his fellow shipmates. Some of them sat in front, some in back, and clearly all of them were not vampires.

"That looks like all of you," the boatman declared, and clapped his hands loudly. He cleared his throat by pounding on his chest, which looked very painful, and scrutinized his suddenly captive audience. "This is where I give you a speech," he announced. "So here it is. I am the boatman. And all of you are beginners."

Everyone looked around, perplexed.

Beginners?

"That wasn't a question. That is what you are. Beginners. Beginners are first year students."

Mutual nods of understanding moved from one bobbing head to another.

"I am Olaf. Of the mariner race. Do any of you know it?"

A young girl raised her hand.

"Yes little girlie."

"Angelica," she said, sharply.

Alex looked over to her.

The girl was petite, with green eyes, and hair as red as a bowl full of cherries. Her jacket, stockings, shoes, and tiny cape, were all in absolute and perfect order.

"Angelica," the man Olaf countered. He was slightly taken aback by her robotic pronunciation. "And what have you heard about the mariners?"

"They are rulers of the wind and sea."

"Ah. Very well put. Very well put indeed. Now. Where are we, you are wondering? Yes?" He looked around and said, "This is the Sea of Giants. Created when the dark races hid from humankind by retreating into Carpathia. Which is where you all live, by the way, in case some of you didn't know."

"It's big," a voice squeaked.

Alex looked around. Below him, sitting on the edge of his suitcase, was a little boy. A *very little* boy. Seven inches tall, in fact. With fluttering wings, shimmering hair, and arms crossed. This was Ariel, a French pixie of the Crystal Forest.

"Yes, it is," Olaf went on, "now all of you *sitttt back-kkk*, and enjoy the sights. If any of you fall overboard, don't forget to scream."

Eyes bulged at this comment.

"I hope he's not serious," Angelica said, alarmingly.

Alex looked at her. "I think he is."

Olaf, with a quick hand, threw off the rope which bound them to the dock, swung up his humongous oar, and slammed the instrument directly into the water. A spray of foam splashed into everyone's faces.

"WE ARE COMING!" the mariner proclaimed, but no one knew who he was talking to.

After a few minutes of nervous silence, and a whole lot of ups and downs, the boat settled into a steady pace.

"My name is Ariel." It was the pixie at Alex's feet, who now hovered in front of him like a hummingbird. "We do not shake hands except with our own kind. We bow instead. That's why I'm bowing."

"Oh," Alex said, and bowed his head. "I'm Alex. Of Hillock Green."

"*Bonjour*. Can I sit on your case?"

"Ugh . . . sure."

"If the wind picks up I can put my legs under the straps."

The Angelica girl, who sat directly across from Alex, raised her chin and asked, "Where's your bat?"

Alex, startled, looked up. The girl with the cherry hair was speaking to him. "Me?" he asked.

"Yes, you. Don't you have a bat? You're a vampire, aren't you?"

"Yes."

Angelica snapped her fingers. Her eyes lit up. "Oh, that's right. You can turn into them. You can turn into a bat?"

All eyes turned to Alex.

"Well?" the girl insisted.

"I can't," Alex replied. "But some can."

The pixie watched the exchange with fascination.

"He's right," another vampire boy offered, from behind.

"Are you sure?" The girl looked puzzled. "That's strange. I read that *all* vampires can turn into bats. I'm sure I read that. Absolutely sure."

"Vampires have different abilities. They're unique to each person." Alex noticed the pixie was staring at him.

Angelica frowned. "I read a history of your race but it didn't say anything about that. I'll have to insist the book be amended. The author probably never met a vampire though, which probably accounts for the inaccuracy."

"They must have," a vampire girl said. She was sitting behind Batcakes.

Angelica shook her head. "This is the first year our kind has gone to school."

"What is *your* kind?" Batcakes asked. He reached over and touched her hair.

"Excuse me!" She slapped his hand away. "That's rude. Don't you have any manners?"

Batcakes gawked, stupefied by the question. "It didn't look like real hair."

"Well it is." Angelica huffed and turned back to the

others, "We're elementals."

Olaf broke in—"All right beginners. Look to your right."

Eyes turned.

A harbor glimmered in the distance, with the pointed peaks of a city, just beyond. Unlike the plain dock they had just come from, Alex noticed this jetty was full of tangled ropes and big steamboats. Peculiar green creatures moved here and there. All of them with long, snake tails.

"What are *those* things?" Angelica asked.

"Ahhhh," Olaf mouthed in admiration. "Lizard folk. Not very nice if you want to sit down with them for a meal—but good fighters."

"Is it a city?" someone else asked.

"Yes." Olaf's white beard fluttered in the wind. "Snake City. The Trading Capital of Carpathia."

Alex made a mental note of the name and pulled a piece of candy from his pocket.

"What's that?" Ariel asked. The candy was half the size of his body.

Alex held it up. "Blood pop."

"Disgusting!" Angelica blurted out.

"Ewwwwwwwww," Ariel squeaked.

Alex couldn't understand what the fuss was about. "It's just a piece of candy," he replied, innocently. In the cemetery of Hillock Green, blood pops, blood soup, blood pudding, as well as an unlimited variety of other foods, were just soooo very common. All the food grew in the fields where the blood trees were planted. And it was all organic! Blood cake was his favorite. "Do you want a bite?"

Alex held the candy out to Angelica.

She shivered and waved her hands. "Yucky."

"I'll take it," Batcakes said.

The pop was beginning to melt. Once you unwrapped them, they never lasted very long. He handed it to Batcakes.

"Wow! Thanks." Batcakes took the dripping gob and plopped it into his mouth.

"That's even worse," Angelica said, her face warping. "Don't you even care that it was in his mouth?! Yuck! He's given you his dirty seconds."

Batcakes shook his head, happily. "I don't mind."

Angelica stared him down. "You have no manners. Do not try to sit next to me at the lunch table!"

Alex wondered if Angelica had already made up her mind who she *would* be sitting next to. The girl turned to Olaf. "Sir? Is it a long way?"

"Yes. Very long. Very, very long. Hold on!"

Abruptly, the boat jerked and smacked against a water swell.

"The edge—" Ariel squealed.

"Look out!" someone yelled.

Water spewed up against the sides.

"If you don't get wet, then you're not in a boat!" Olaf announced.

Alex was thinking it was supposed to be the other

way around.

Suddenly the boat crashed against another rising tide.

Angelica shrieked.

"HOLD ON!"

Alex tried to grab something, but there was nothing to grab.

The beginners flew to the bottom of the boat—capes on capes, suitcases flying—and landed in a very large pile, one on top of the other.

After a few seconds, everyone uncurled themselves and looked around.

"Are we alive?" someone asked.

Angelica blew strands of hair out of her face. Her voice was sarcastic. "I'm not!"

"That was fun!" Batcakes proclaimed.

Olaf, who was whistling happily to himself, didn't seem to notice.

8

PELAGIA

*W*hen the boat came into the waters of Atlantica, Olaf turned to the beginners and asked, "What do you see?"

Everyone looked out and into the blackness beyond. Strange sounds echoed in the dark, but nothing was *visible*. At least not to Alex anyway. Only rippling water and the faint outline of cliffs in the distance.

Alex tried to use his vampire vision.

"What's wrong?" Batcakes probed, for he noticed Alex's furrowed face.

"Nothing, I just—"

Angelica cut him off. "I see them!"

The spontaneous statement sent everyone to the edge of the boat.

Angelica squealed. "There! Over there!"

Alex could feel someone trying to climb over him.

The boat tipped.

"Wait!" Olaf barked. He smashed his oar into the water on the opposite side of the vessel. Luckily he knew how to balance and steer. "Warning! Give me warning!"

But there was no time for warnings! Oh no. Things were moving—something was happening. Just below the surface there were creatures darting and dashing and hurrying.

"Where?!"

"What are they?"

"There . . ."

"—see, see!"

The beginners didn't know it, but these were the magical faeries of the water land, born and raised in castles, and trained for battle.

"What are they?" a vampire girl asked.

"Atlanticans," Olaf annunciated. But that was all he said, for he was concentrating on guiding the boat, and the waters of Atlantica were especially treacherous.

"Atlanticans," whispered Alex.

"Nine fathom deep!" and then the boat turned. Olaf held the oar steadily. "But they are not to be trifled with. Shark family."

"I guess I won't go swimming," Angelica drawled.

"Can they speak?" Alex asked. He tried to look deeper into the water.

"Of course," Olaf answered.

Just then, one of the creatures erupted from the surface, somersaulted in the air, and crashed back into the water.

"Trés bien!" Ariel shrilled happily.

Another glided towards the boat and pulled herself up to the rim.

Alex found himself staring directly into her big, fishy eyes.

There were many things he noticed about her. Her face, though covered in scales, was very beautiful, and speckled with silver dots. Her eyes twinkled, like Carpathian marbles, and on top of her head, instead of hair, a fin protruded. It trailed down her neck to the middle of her back. Alex naturally assumed she was a mermaid, which she wasn't.

"Are you going to Witchwood?" she asked, as she brushed her fin (as though it was her hair) with her hand, and blinked. "It is very dangerous there this time of year."

Olaf answered before Alex could speak. "No no no my little one. We travel to The Carpathian Academy."

She turned to Alex. "I am Pelagia. You are familiar to me."

"Me?" Alex asked in surprise.

Pelagia nodded smoothly.

"I'm Alex."

"Vambarey," she purred, "of Hillock Green."

She knew him! But how? It was impossible. He had never met any other creatures (until now) besides vampires. "How do you know me?"

Pelagia removed her necklace. It was a delicate string, with the smallest stone at the end. A spider's thread of silk. "Keep this," she told him.

Alex held out his hand as Pelagia dropped the necklace into his open palm.

"Thank you, but—" He stammered. The necklace was beautiful. Fragile. He was about to tell her he couldn't keep it, but everything was happening so fast.

"For a time of need," she said. "But will you forget?" Her large penetrating eyes looked into his. "Please don't forget."

Alex answered quickly. "No. I won't. I won't forget."

She smiled. "I am to help you. And someone like you."

"Me," spouted Batcakes, and he smiled between two jolly cheeks. "I hope."

Pelagia glided, effortlessly, beside them.

Olaf continued to row.

"How do you know?" Alex asked. He leaned over the edge of the boat. If he could just swim with her!

She looked up. "The Oracle told me of it. Goodbye!"

"Wait!" Alex yelped. "Come back!"

But Pelagia had already submerged, and was disappearing into the depths.

"Over there little ones," Olaf called out, and pointed.

In the distance, a large iceberg protruded from the dropsy water. It was the strangest iceberg Alex had ever seen, that was for sure. Mostly because it was so tall and narrow.

"That is how you know Atlantica!" Olaf announced. His voice was as majestic as the wind.

Everyone watched as the tiny boat moved up to the mountainous silver spectacle.

Suddenly a gruff voice broke the silence—

"Ow!"

Alex looked over his shoulder. Something was moving behind him.

Louder: "Ugh!"

Alex spun in his seat.

A tarp, which was in the area behind the rows, moved. Whatever was beneath was grunting too.

A second later, Otis Fluff emerged and stretched his short, muscled arms. "Are we there yet?" he asked.

Alex couldn't believe that anything could *sleep* through all the ruckus.

Batcakes laughed.

Everyone else gawked. This didn't seem like a boy at all. More like a monster. His arms were thick, as well as his hands, and his body was dark blue. Circular volcanoes speckled his skin from head to toe, and a small cloak hung from his neck. Also, his head was large, and he had short, spiky ears.

Ariel retreated to the other side of the boat.

"We're not there yet," Alex said, in response to this boy-thing. "We've just gone through Atlantica."

What was this creature?

Alex held out his hand to shake. "I'm Alex."

The boy shook it, and yawned right after. "Otis," he said.

Angelica, slightly miffed, said, "You're introducing

yourself to everyone, aren't you?"

Alex ignored her.

"What are you?" Batcakes asked. "I mean . . ."

Otis stared at him, puzzled. He scratched a few hairs between his ears.

"He's a gargoyle," Angelica said firmly. "Isn't that what you are?"

Alex noticed the boy had very little hair and ridges for eyebrows. "Oh yes. Gargoyle," he replied, and rubbed his eyes. "What time is it anyway? Is it time for lunch?"

Angelica turned to Alex. She wasn't at all interested in gargoyles. "Put it on," she said.

Alex was too stunned by Otis (being a gargoyle, after all) to realize what she meant.

"Put the necklace on," she insisted. "You'll lose it otherwise."

The necklace! How could he have forgotten?!

Alex lifted it over his head and placed it around his neck.

"Do you feel any different?" Batcakes asked.

"No. I don't think so."

"ARRIVAL MOST SOUND!" Olaf blared.

The boat moved to a rocky reef where another wooden wharf extended into the water.

Everyone clutched the rim of the boat—except for Otis—and tried to stay in their seats.

Olaf guided the ship skillfully. Once at the pier, he tossed a rope over a small wooden pole, and secured the craft. "FOLLOW THE STAIRCASE! UP!"

Unsure if this was a cue, everyone waited.

Olaf changed his tone. Instead of yelling, he spoke normally, which was much more agreeable to Alex's ears. "This is it. We're here. You can get off the boat."

This seemed to do the trick, and the beginners gathered up their suitcases and bags.

Once the entire boat was empty, the gaggle of students turned back to wave goodbye.

Olaf stood at the helm, with the vessel's dragons head behind him. He held up one strong hand to them. It was the mariner's way of saying goodbye.

"Call me Olaf!" he told them, "and be merry! For tomorrow you will no longer be little. And I will be Olaf no more!"

With that proclamation, he swiftly unhooked the boat.

Alex watched as the sea grabbed up the vessel, and pulled Olaf into the night.

9

SCARECROWS

"*You* can still see the tip of that rock," Otis pronounced joyfully. He was referring to the Atlantican rock. In the distance, like a magnificent tower, it protruded up from the water.

Otis and Alex stood at the end of the pier. The rest of their shipmates had already gone on ahead.

"I didn't know it was a rock," Alex said.

"It's a marker rock. If you're reading a map you use it as a reference point. Or if you're flying."

Alex's cape rustled in the wind. He noticed it was beginning to rain. "What do you think those are?"

In the distance, star-speckled lights hung in the air. They glowed in one mass like a group of dragonflies.

"Maybe a city or hamlet. Or just houses. Someday I want to live in a really modern house, with a whole bunch of light, and tons of glass windows."

Alex pivoted and looked at Otis. He liked this boy, even if he was kind of strange. "You don't like caves?"

"Not really."

Alex laughed. "I don't know if you're going to be a very good gargoyle then."

"I always felt like I was something else, but I never knew what." Otis turned and raised his clawed hand to the west. "Transopolis is over there. You know, the vampire city."

"Vampire City?"

"You haven't heard of it?"

Alex shook his head 'no'.

"Really?"

Alex stared at the flares in the darkness. He could just make out the tips of the battlements, and the rising spires.

"It's very dangerous," Otis went on, "that's what my mum told me."

"I want to go there," Alex said.

"When I first saw you I thought that's where you were from."

"Really? I wish I was."

Otis shrugged. "I don't know much about it. I only know about the caves. I've never been anywhere else."

Alex shook his head. "I just never realized the Green was so small." He turned back to Otis. "That's where I'm from. Hillock Green."

Otis watched Alex closely. This boy was really smart. Otis quickly looked at his claws to see if they were clean. This vampire boy would *never* be his friend if he couldn't keep his claws clean.

Alex scanned the surroundings. The platform was empty.

"I think we're supposed to go up there," Otis suggested.

At the end of the wharf, a staircase cut into the mountain in a zig-zag, with a bright yellow rope as leader.

Otis moved to the first step. A wooden stick rested on his shoulder, with a sack on the end. "Do you want me to stay with you?"

Alex smiled. "No, I'm coming."

A burst of thunder roared over them, followed by a thin sheet of rain.

Alex grabbed his suitcase and ran to where Otis stood.

"It's pretty steep. If you stay next to me, I'll grab you if you fall," Otis said.

"Thanks. I'll be all right."

Otis's eyes lit up. "You can turn into a bat," he said gleefully. "I should've known that." Otis had been sleeping when Angelica had first brought up the whole 'bat' thing.

"I can't, actually."

Otis eyed Alex quizzically. "Oh." He paused, and tapped his chin twice with his claw. "Interesting. I guess my mum isn't right about everything."

What a funny thing to say, Alex thought.

"Well, if you slip, I can grab you with these," he said,

and held up his thick claws. "I'm real strong."

Alex believed him.

"You go first," Otis said.

"Okay."

They both climbed.

It took about five minutes to reach the top, but once there, a colossal creature was waiting. Her name was Wilhelmina Warderton Witt.

"Taking your time," she said haughtily. "Or just seeing the sights?"

Now this Wilhelmina beastie was a very, very large worm, with little arms and a very funny face. She had a purse which hung around her massive neck and a walking stick too. On top of her worm head sat an eensy weensy witch hat.

Otis and Alex froze. Neither of them had ever seen a worm witch before.

"Sorry," Alex finally managed to get out.

"Well, you made it. Obviously. Even though you could have fallen down the cliff and died. Or been swept away in the waves, or possibly taken by a harpy without anyone knowing. Hence, where would that leave you? And where would I be, for that matter, for I would be the one to be blamed!"

Alex mumbled another 'sorry' while Otis just glared, bulgy-eyed.

"Well, you're here now. Come on." She turned and slithered off her rock.

Alex and Otis followed her.

Otis poked Alex to get his attention. He put a thumb in each ear, wiggled his fingers, and stuck his tongue out at her.

Alex laughed.

Wilhelmina did not see any of this, mind you, for she was sliding—like all worms do—down the walkway.

"This is the dead pumpkin field. If you need to go somewhere," she said, "sometimes they'll help you."

Alex looked around. *Who would help them?*

The field Wilhelmina was referring to stretched off on both sides of the path, indefinitely. It was filled with very large pumpkins. Not orange, happy ones, mind you, but weird, dark, ugly ones, all covered in warts. Above them, on tall posts, scary scarecrows swayed in the breeze, with tipped down floppy hats, thick boots, shiny black gloves (which was very weird), and each with a scythe fastened to the back of their beam. The blade was large, sharp, and sickled.

"This place doesn't look very friendly," Alex said.

Otis nodded. "You're right."

Wilhelmina stopped. She leaned on her walking stick.

Alex asked, "Are you all right?"

Wilhelmina's worm body was so huge Alex thought she might be tuckered out.

"Yes," she snapped, "of course. What a silly question." Wilhelmina did not look at him, but instead sifted through her purse. The miniscule handbag hung over her entire body on a chain.

Finally, she pulled out a small cylinder with one hand, held up a mirror with the other, and started applying a very bright lipstick to her balloon sized lips. Color: orange.

Yuck.

Alex seized the moment and slipped into the field. His creeping skills were pretty good, even if his mother had heard him the night before.

"Where are you going?" Otis whispered.

"There," he said, and pointed to one of the scarecrows.

"I thought you said this place looked scary?"

"It does. But I want to see one up close."

Unlike Alex, Otis was *not* good at creeping. His feet crunched against the straw loudly as he attempted incognito.

Alex reached one of the scarecrows and stopped. Now he could get a really good look at it. The scarecrow was wearing a red and black checkered shirt, which he couldn't see before, and heavy black boots. Everything—the gloves, the pants, the shirt, and the large brimmed hat—were covered in dirt. Throughout the body, spiky straw stuck out of holes.

Both of them glanced up to the darkened face.

"You can't see the face," Otis whispered.

"I know," Alex said. "I want to see it though. Come on—"

A wind whistled through the field.

"No you don't!" Wilhelmina barked—out of nowhere—and grabbed Alex's arm. "Is this how the entire school term is going to be? With both of you wandering off?" She towered over them, now even more frightening than before, her neck suddenly curling out from her thick worm body. "I think the both of you are going to be hooligans! Trouble making hooligans!"

"We just wanted to see them," Alex said, his voice deflated.

"Unless you're using them, you don't want to. And even *then* you don't want to."

What did she mean by that?

"Come along now. I don't want them holding the train for us." Wilhelmina poked Alex with her stick and shuffled them back towards the path.

Otis turned to Alex and said, "Use them for what?"

Alex shook his head. "I don't know. But I want to find out."

"I'm surprised they let you in," Wilhelmina clucked.

"Who?" Otis asked.

"The scarecrows, of course. My goodness, child, are you obtuse?"

"Why wouldn't they?" Alex asked.

"Not just anyone can go into the fields." She looked down to them, her eyebrows raised. "Curious, I should say. They must have wanted to examine you. For what reason, I have absolutely no idea." She thought about this for a moment, and then confirmed it in her mind with a nod of her head. "Yes. They needed to look at you, that is for sure. But for what reason I'll never know!"

Otis didn't understand a word the worm was saying.

65

Alex, on the other hand, wondered. Why *had* they let them into the field? What exactly did they need to look at anyway? Him?

He looked back over his shoulder. The withered pumpkins sat in the dark fields, their forms round and ominous against a backdrop of stars. The silhouettes of scarecrows hanging above them—

One of the scarecrows tipped its head up.

Alex jumped. "One of them just moved! I just saw—"

Wilhelmina cut him off. "We're here."

"But—!" Alex proclaimed.

"No buts! Buts are going to make you miss the train."

Two stone pillars stretched up in front of them, their tops blazing fire. Beyond, another path stretched and curved to the left.

"I just saw one of the—"

"Never mind!" the worm screeched.

"But—"

"What did I say about buts!" Wilhelmina swung around. "Hooligans! I can already see it! Hooligans!"

Alex was about to protest again, but figured there was no use.

The worm jerked her stick and pointed. "Through there," she said.

"I don't like fire," Otis said weakly.

"Well it doesn't care a toot about you," Wilhelmina piped.

Alex could see, just beyond the pillars, glowing rocks lining the path.

Otis didn't move.

Perturbed, Wilhelmina snapped, "Gargoyles are not afraid of fire. Vampires are. Besides, look how high up the fire is? Far too high to touch the likes of you." She slithered back a few feet and bopped Otis on the head with her cane. "I *refuse* to wait here for two hooligans. If you don't hurry up, you're going to miss the boat." She wormed towards the pillars, but soon realized that neither Alex, nor Otis, had budged. She turned, shook her cane in the air and screamed, "Are you two listening to MEEEEEE!!!!?"

"We're going!" Alex exclaimed.

The worm shook her finger at Alex. "Don't you *dare* talk back to me batboy."

"I'm not. Come on." Alex gave Otis a little push.

Otis walked forward, but now clutched his rucksack to his chest.

Alex looked over to him. "Did she say boat or train?"

"I think . . . boat. But she first said train. I think."

Alex shook his head. *All this just to get to school?! What next?*

Otis, with a roll of his furrowed gargoyle eyes, said, "Humans have it easy. All they have to do is get on a bus."

10

THE GIANT'S TRAIN

Alex and Otis soon learned there was no boat. Wilhelmina was just using that as a figure of speech. But there was a train. All the cabooses stretched back from the front locomotive and into a humongous, dark tunnel.

The 12 foot tall conductor stood waiting at the front. He had a face that looked like a rock and a checkerboard cap. A cigarette dangled from his down-turned mouth and he leaned against the front train car with a newspaper in hand.

"We're going to get stepped on," Otis yelled out.

There was so much activity next to the locomotive, you pretty much had to yell. The hissing trains and pounding shoes of the giants reverberated throughout the tunnel.

"You will *not* get stepped on! Giants are well aware of the school term. Our caboose is in the middle," Wilhelmina said. "Now come along."

Wilhelmina slithered towards the front of the train. Alex and Otis trotted behind her.

"Do you have any friends going to school?"

Otis thought about it for a second, and said, "My mum told me there are two boys going from the Hungarian Caves, but I've never met them."

"What's your cave like?"

Otis lit up. "Oh, very interesting. We have hieroglyphics in ours."

"What's that?"

"Cave writing."

They moved out of the clearing and into the dark mouth of the passage. Cones of light shot down from perfectly round lamps, suspended one after the other by tall black poles.

"There's your silverline," Wilhelmina said. She pointed her stick to a train car. It was situated between two giant compartments, and looked like a shiny toy sitting between mountains. Very sleek.

Wilhelmina slithered to a stop. "This is where I see you off," she mouthed, with her big orange lips, "good luck." And with that, she wriggled away.

A sudden blast of steam sent Alex's cape into the air.

Otis stared at the futuristic tallyho in front of them. "It looks so small compared to the other ones."

Alex said, "I guess the other ones are just for the giants."

The two boys ran to the entrance of the first cab, which hissed as they approached, and dashed up the metal steps to the main seating area.

"Let's go to the back," Otis said.

They both passed Batcakes, who was sitting in the front row. "Hey guys," he chirped, before turning his attention back to a red apple. A green-eyed girl had given it to him.

"Go ahead and eat it," she encouraged. She said this while circling her hands over the top of its sprightly stem.

Batcakes looked up to them with a pained expression. He was very susceptible to suggestion, the girl was pretty, *and* he was hungry. Not a good combination for Batcakes.

Alex and Otis plopped down next to Angelica in the back of the caboose.

"What happened to you two?" she asked.

"We got sidetracked," Alex replied.

Otis took his bag and opened it. He withdrew a small black case and took out a pair of glasses.

Angelica turned to him. "You wear glasses? That's curious. Gargoyles are supposed to have excellent vision."

Alex lifted his suitcase and tossed it into the overhead luggage nook.

"Not when you're young," he said. "We don't get our vision until the middle years."

Alex fell into his seat and looked out the window. Slowly, the train was beginning to move. The wheels creaking against their metal encasings.

"Finally," Angelica declared.

Ariel zipped to the window. "I want to go home," he said. "What can we learn at this school that the forest can't teach us?"

No one had an answer.

Otis, out of the blue, said, "This train is really modern."

There was so much ruckus and flurry and chaos, not to mention giants—Alex hadn't taken note of the interior of the 'silverline', as Wilhelmina had called it.

The core of the train's chamber had chrome racks where you could place your bags, sleek seats with cushions, and shiny blue and black trim. Plus it had nice clean carpet and glistening windows.

Alex turned to Otis and asked, "Is this what they call modern?"

Otis nodded. "Sure," and he brought his voice down to a whisper, "but there's only one book about it in our library. I've checked it out a dozen times. It's a human thing."

This piqued Alex's interest. "Really?"

"They created it. The modern thing. They call it a *style*."

"Style?"

"Yeah, like a way of setting things in a room. We have rock furniture in our cave. My mom isn't big on style. But they're comfortable rocks. The book had to be from the humans because they don't have any rocks in their houses."

"Maybe it's a vampire book."

"No, vampire houses always look like castles."

Alex thought about this. Did everyone's house in Hillock Green look like a castle?

"Don't they?" Otis asked.

"I guess. I never thought about it before."

"Anyway, my older brother's friend told me about it. 'Modern' and 'style' are both human words."

Alex got excited. "Well, if there is a human book in your library that means someone *got* it from the humans. Which means they must have met one."

Otis shrugged. "Maybe. I just like the pictures though."

Angelica kicked Otis in the leg.

"Ow!"

"What are you two whispering about?"

"Rocks," Otis said.

"Rocks? What about them?"

"We were just talking about the rock formations in my cave and—"

Angelica interrupted him, "Borrrrring. Never mind."

The windows had fogged up and the wheels were swooshing.

"I wish we weren't in a cave," she said, "you can't see anything."

Alex's mind drifted off. He began to wonder about Ariel's comment. What was the purpose of going to school anyway? Everything you needed to learn was at home, wasn't it? Hillock Green had a huge library. They had doctors and scholars and everything else too. This was just going to be a big waste of time.

But what he didn't know was that—yes—he *was* the vampire boy that Pelagia would help. And he *was* the boy that would one day search the rocks of the Iron Land.

And if Alex could hear the rest (as though his destiny was in a song), it would go something like this:

He will do this, and that, and so much more!
He will cross land and sea.
Some say he will meet the mermaids
while having tea.

What beautiful magic is in the vast unknown:
A ride on a Giant's train in the dark.
And the ringing, tinging, singing,
Of Amelia Lark.

II

THE MAGUS

The train did not grind to a stop, but sailed effort-lessly to a seamless finish, and gave off a tiny toot.

"Are we here?" Someone asked.

They were, and a moment later, the spaceship-like doors slid open and the students tumbled out with their belongings in tow.

Soon they were walking up a wide set of steps (in a very large castle), and towards the main courtyard of the Carpathian Academy.

A cape flapped into Alex's face just as he noticed a will-o'-the-wisp. The purple light was in an adjoin-ing corridor and bouncing up and down. Alex quickly pushed the cloak out of his face. But, by the time he did, it was gone.

A vampire named Hadrian led them. He was tall, with big muscles, and short curly hair. Draping from his neck to the middle of his back hung a short gold cape.

Alex peered anxiously between the jouncing heads in front of him.

When they reached the courtyard, Alex could see a tall vampire standing on a platform at the end of the quad. Behind him, a variety of teachers sat on stone seats. Like Alex, he too had pure white hair, except for a black streak which ran through the center of his head. His cape stretched to the stone platform below and sparkled.

"That's the Magus," Angelica whispered.

"I know," Alex replied. He was trying to get a better view.

Hadrian stopped, unexpectedly, a little way into the crowd, and turned. "Halt please! Stay where you are and the Magus will greet you."

Alex surveyed his fellow students. Most of them were gathered in groups, while others chit-chatted about what was to come.

Throughout the courtyard, statues were set, and in the center, a colossal fountain flowed with clear green water.

Alex liked that especially. At the top, five stone bats were entwined with the edges of their wings touching. Glowing water spurted out from the center of their united circle.

Many of the students were not just standing, but sitting together on the various stone tables. All chattering in a flish-flush of enthusiasm.

A few girls squealed.

Hadrian raised a clenched fist in the air. He boomed—"QUIEEEEEEEET!"

And everyone did—immediately.

The Magus waited for the crowd to simmer down. The four teachers seated behind him were: Mrs. Philpotts, Professor Mab, Professor Ticora, and Mr. Warwick. Also, just below the stone dais, a piano had been wheeled out into the courtyard. The music teacher, Mrs. Chord, sat on a small stool in front of it. Her hair was pulled up in a tight grey bun and her purple dress flowed out behind her.

With a simple nod from the Magus, Mrs. Chord began to play. It was a short, bright introduction, and quite cheery. She finished with the pluck of two black keys.

Applause ensued, and then died down after the Magus raised his arms. His voice was sharp and concise. "I am Magus Whitlock. Welcome to the Carpathian Academy. You will first be escorted to your wings. All the wings—pun intended—are divided into age groups, and that is where you will be placed."

"He's scary," Otis said.

Alex smiled. "I like him."

Otis tipped his head sideways.

The Magus continued: "We have two new races this year who have joined the Carpathian Alliance. The elemental race, and the pixie race. Please welcome them." The students clapped. "AND, after you have become acquainted with your new friends—explore! The castle is *yours* for this night, and classes begin on the morrow. Also, so no one gets lost—or worse—there will be no admittance to certain sections—including the school store."

Alex turned to Otis. "There's a store?"

"It's supposed to be huge," Otis replied, eagerly. "It has candy from all over the world." He paused, and went on, "I even heard that it has *human* candy. I'm hoping it's not just a rumor though. They put your study books on hold there too."

"Really?" Alex was suddenly troubled. He said, "My parents didn't give me any coin."

Otis waved a claw. "You don't need it. Your parents give the store your tab in advance. It's all set up. They have a leprechaun too."

"A leprechaun?" Alex was amazed. He had seen drawings of them—little funny men at the end of night rainbows, but never one in person. "Are you sure?"

"Sure I'm sure."

The Magus held his hands out. "Now," he said, "for this year's riddle."

There was an excited pause—

This, Alex knew about. Each wing—usually around fifteen students—competed each year to solve the Magus Riddle. The mind boggler was always imparted at the beginning of the term, and for the rest of the year everyone tried to figure it out. The prize was always a highly desired magical item.

The riddle was announced, and it went like this:

In the night gallery
of the voivode,
A clever woman sits.
Beside her might be
the key to all,
But if not,
then why not quit?

There, where the wind blows hot and fierce,
A single flower grows.
Protected by a king,
Of the Ozymandias ring,
The dead red river flows.

Bring it back and win the prize,
But is it worth the price?
It helps all little ones to be,
Healthy, happy, alive—and free.

The Magus broke off, and took a moment. "For those of you scribbling—admirable. But the riddle is hanging in the Grand Hall. You can copy it down there." Which, of course, halted the frenzied notations. All eyes shot back up to him. "This night only, dinner will be served in your wings. But before dinner, and after, the castle is yours. To explore, meet, and to start your new year on a note of exploration. The curfew bell will let you know when you must return to your wings. Any student roaming the halls after curfew will be dealt with by the hall monitors." He smiled and let his hands unfurl to the crowd. "So *enjoy*. When the sessions begin tomorrow, they will not be easy. But do remember, no matter how difficult it might become," and he waved to the teachers behind him, "we believe in your minds, *and* your hearts."

With that, he bowed his head to the wide-eyed students, and finished with, "And now, I bid you good night."

12

The Difference

Between a

Wizard and a Witch

Alex and Otis found that they were housed in the Walachia Wing—boys only—and now were being led, with a small group of others, to their dormitory.

Their escort, Goblin Greg, walked in front. Thin black hair sprouted from his goblin head, a large round belly stuck out of his belt, and huge legs ended in wide, bare feet.

"None of you know what it is like to be riddled with back aches and stomach pains. Everything I eat. *Everything!* Every single morsel upsets my stomach, which starts to hurt my back, and after that hurts *everything*."

This beast of a Greg was visibly upset, with his goblin face all contorted. He paused as he ambled down the long hall to the Walachia wing while clutching his belly. "I have been adding and taking away and adding and taking away, and now I have identified one of the problems!" After the stomach clutch, he shuffled forward, but did not stop talking, "It is wheat! I had a piece—quite large—of bread this morning and my back immediately began to ache! So it must be wheat. It must be! I can think of no other solution. And now, besides all the other things I can no longer eat, I am barred from eating wheat as well. No wheat MEANS no bread. No bread! Can you believe this?! And of course the doctors can do nothing. I see them over and over and over. But there is never—*never* an answer. They always say it is something you are eating. I know that! For goblin sake! Don't they think I know that? But no answers are ever put forth to solve the problem. It is a curse I must live with. A terrible and most horrible curse. And, all the while, I am tortured by having to watch you little ones eat anything and absolutely everything you please. And there I stand . . . starving. Horribly starving. Quite to death. Look at me. Have you ever seen a goblin so skinny? I ask you that? Have you?"

To Alex, Goblin Greg looked quite plump. But, in all fairness, he had never seen a goblin before.

Otis whispered, "He doesn't look starving to me."

Alex laughed, but quickly hid the smile with his cape.

"Here we are," Goblin Greg said, despondently. He stopped at a large wooden door with strange metal hoops. The rings hung from the middle of the door and trailed down to the bottom. "I will not be staying to watch you eat your wonderful supper, that is for sure."

Goblin Greg grabbed the knocker angrily. The knocker was so huge only a goblin (or something larger perhaps) could open it.

Not to worry though. Beneath the huge knocker, another knocker was placed. And then another, and another. All the way down there were door knockers, and at the end, even a door knocker for a pixie.

It swung open.

Goblin Greg stood at the threshold with his arms crossed. Though completely agitated, he still urged the beginners into the room, "Go in, go in. First come, first serve for the beds."

The boys dashed into the Walachia wing.

"It will be your resting place," he goblined, for some of the boys had already vanished through the archway into the next chamber, "for the rest of the year!"

Let me explain. The wing consisted of beds, side by side, and each in a separate compartment. At the end of the chamber an arched doorway led to a second room, which served as the lounge and reading alcove. The two areas made up the entirety of the Walachia wing.

In the center of each chamber stood a fireplace, with carved stone faces around its grate, and a chimney that twisted up.

While everyone examined the bed-sits, Goblin Greg shuffled to the fireplace.

Otis didn't know where to look first.

"What about the one in the corner?" Alex asked. He pointed to the end of the chamber, just by the archway to the next room.

"Let's fly!" was Otis's answer, and they both hurried to the undiscovered compartment.

Alex threw the drapery aside as Otis ran in.

The compartment revealed a coffin on one side, and a pillowy cushion (covering the floor) on the other.

"This looks good," Alex said. He set his suitcase on the floor. "What do you think?"

Otis moved into the chamber. "Definitely. And there's no straw on my side, so that's good."

Alex noted that the coffin in the room was quite plain, and made of simple wood.

It didn't matter though. Not really. Alex knew it was only for the one night. The faculty always arranged for the vampire children to have their coffins transported from home, as a courtesy.

"We can unpack later. I want to see the school before dinner."

"Mine is like a human bed," Otis said.

"Really?" Alex went to him.

"Did you know that humans have lumps they put their heads on."

"Lumps?"

Otis nodded.

"What kind of lumps?"

"They're gooey and big and they hide their face underneath it when they sleep."

"Maybe the lumps are like our cushions. See how the cushions are sewn into the coffin."

Otis walked over to the coffin and peered inside. "Maybe."

Alex mulled. "I know they have all sorts of weird habits though."

"They do. My brother was the one that told me about the lumps. He also said they have this ugly ball that sits in the sky and a *day*. Kind of like our darkday I guess. But the ugly ball can burn them, or blind them. The moon doesn't stay out all the time like ours either. It hides from the sun and when darkness comes, it feels that it's all right to come out of its hiding place." He paused and his nose wrinkled up. "But my brother likes to tell stories."

Alex was about to answer Otis's semi-question, but decided against it. He suddenly wondered if the humans did, in fact, own dragons called Aero-planes.

But enough of that. He signaled to Otis, "Come on. Let's check out the school."

"What about dinner?" Otis's mind was always on food.

Alex didn't care two bats about food when there was so much to explore, but he knew Otis would think otherwise. "Well. Dinner is in about an hour. So we'll go out, come back, and go out again."

That was the correct response. Otis smiled. "Good.

Because they didn't have any snacks on the boat or the train."

The Walachia boys were now made up of Otis, Alex, and a small group of others. They walked down the central hall and towards the main courtyard. Dinner was over, and now everyone had free reign—at least for the remaining hours before curfew.

"You *can't* see it because there is magic preventing it," Edwald announced to the gang. This was Edwald Trowbridge, who was taller than most of the boys, and a Druid. He had fine, silky blonde hair and skin that was caramel colored. His hair was a cool shag and his brown eyes were unusually large. He wore no hat (like many of the other Druid beginners), but still donned the classic druid cape, which was aqua blue and covered in gold stars.

Edwald was referring to the ceiling in the hallway, which was invisible. "So they make the ceiling invisible so you can see the stars and the moon. Just in case you want to identify them."

"What are you?" The vampire boy Klytus asked, with genuine curiosity. He was from the Hun province, and had jet black hair. "Are you a vampire?"

An orange bat flew by.

"No," Edwald said. He seemed to be offended. "I am not."

Otis clomped beside Alex. He offered the answer to Klytus: "He's a Druid. Tree people."

"You're wizards then?" Alex asked. There had been many of these boys and girls in the courtyard, and on the train as well. Alex hadn't spoken to any of them until now.

"He wishes he was a wizard," a different boy said.

Edwald ignored the comment. "No. There is a wizard school though. With the humans." He fluttered his hand to indicate a far-away place. "Somewhere out there. I don't know how you get to it. But everyone knows about it. It's famous."

"Really?" Klytus asked.

"Of course it is!" Edwald looked down to Klytus, who was shorter. "Are you kidding? Everybody knows the name of the wizard school. Even the *humans* know about it. It's called . . . " His face bunched up as he tried to recall the name. "It's called . . it's . . . I can't believe I can't remember." Alex could see him getting upset. "Oh puckers!" he exclaimed, which made everyone laugh. "I know the name. It's right on the tip of my hat . . It's— something to do with a pig and a wart."

Otis stared at Edwald. "A pig and a mole?"

"No," Edwald corrected. He gave Otis a sharp look. "I *said* a pig and *wart*. Not a mole."

"My cousin had a wart once," Otis offered happily.

Klytus's eyes lit up. "Really?!"

Edwald shook his head. Somehow everyone was getting *way* off the subject. "That isn't—"

Thrilled by the topic, Pennybrown interrupted, "We had a dwarf pig that got a wart."

Pennyrown had choppy brown hair and an oval face. He was a druid as well, like Edwald, and had a patchwork cape.

Otis moved closer to Pennybrown. "A dwarf pig! Those are great."

"You should have seen that wart on that pig! It got so big it was like a Niminy flower." Pennybrown held up his hands to indicate the size of a large round ball.

"Witches get warts," someone interjected, "I think."

Klytus made a face, "Yuck," and stuck out his tongue.

Edwald finally got back into the conversation. "I think you're *all* missing the point here."

Pennybrown didn't hear Edwald at all. No one did. "What I want to know is—what's the difference between a wizard and a witch anyway?"

The question diverted Edwald from figuring out the name of the wizard school. "It's easy stupid," he said, angrily, "wizards are boys and witches are girls."

Alex was still questioning the difference between a druid and a wizard. Forget about the difference between a wizard and a witch! In the pictures he had seen, druids and wizards all seemed to have the same cloaks, and the same clothing too.

"Anyway, they're different," Edwald said. "We're all different."

So far, Alex noticed that most of the students were either vampires or druids, with a few other races mixed in. There were no other gargoyles besides Otis that he had seen, and Ariel seemed to be the only pixie.

"Anyway, back to what I was saying," Edwald said. "Druids aren't wizards. We live in the forest. In the *trees*."

"Can you fly?" Otis asked. He was peering at this boy now—Edwald Trowbridge—from beneath his gargoyle brows.

"Of course not," Edwald replied. "Don't be deranged."

Deranged?

Otis seemed disappointed.

"But we can do some magic," Edwald articulated.

The group had found their way to the main court-yard and had stopped at a large, circular stone table.

Alex examined Edwald's manner. There was some-thing very *light* about this boy. Alex was a fast runner, but he had a feeling he wouldn't be able to catch Edwald Trowbridge in a race.

"Magic!" Otis clapped his hands loudly, which made some of the vampires wince, and said, "Show us."

"I can't. I haven't learned any," he returned, "—yet." After he made sure all eyes were on him, he continued with, "Besides, that's why we're all here. To find out what our powers are and save the world."

Now the Walachia group had only been sort of paying attention before. Listening, but at the same time looking around too. So as soon as Edwald proclaimed the 'save the world' part, he got everyone's attention.

What had he said? Save the world?!

Edwald stood with his arms crossed, like a king, and peered at Alex, Otis, Pennybrown, Klytus, Ariel, and all the rest. Then he laughed and said, "I'm was just kidding about saving the world. Jeez."

Which made all the boys exhale in relief, with a big humongous sigh.

But listen.

Maybe it's true.

13

DELETER

"*You* are not listening to me Alex Vambarey, and we just met." As soon as Agatha (everyone called her Aggy) saw Alex in the hall, she immediately introduced herself. She had spotted him once in the Hillock Green grocery store, and henceforth pestered her parents about why he had white hair.

Alex noticed there were a lot more bats now and they seemed to be flying helter-skelter above them. His mind drifted as she talked, and kept going back to the humans. What were they like? Did they celebrate every Halloween at the great Wingding?

"I am listening," he insisted.

Aggy was a remarkably petite girl, with her hair woven in a tight ponytail. Her dress was grey and her black stockings stretched down to a set of yellow shoes. A spider pendant was pinned to her dress strap, and the legs stretched out over her shoulder. "This is my friend," she had said, referring to the broach. The body of the insect was a red ruby, and when hit with direct light, it bedazzled the eye.

Alex wondered if Otis had found his destination. After dinner, Otis spontaneously remembered someone named Gargoyle Dan, who was famous for one reason or another, and ran off to find the school's bell tower.

"Good. Because all of this is important," Aggy went on, with a voice full of spunk, "very important."

"I'm listening. I promise."

Aggy stopped in front of a long hallway. She pointed to the top of the entrance. The arched stone met in a point, and at the top, a sign read: Eventide Hall.

"This is our area," Aggy told him.

Alex looked around. The halls were beginning to empty.

"Do you want to see this or not?"

Alex about-faced. "I do. For sure."

"All right. Come on." Aggy walked to the first cabinet. She touched the glass with her fingers. "This is our history. Vampire history. Everyone else has their own hall. Except the gargoyles, I think. I guess their stuff is up in the bell tower or something. Anyway, you can trace all sorts of things in these cabinets. It's really amazing. If you look hard enough you'll probably find your parents in here somewhere. A picture, I mean. I don't know if you know it, but. . . the most famous vampire photographer. . . well, I think he has a son too, lives in *our* cemetery. He's taken a lot of these pictures. Did you know that?"

Alex didn't.

"Well he is definitely in *our* cemetery. Which makes Hillock Green special. All the races come to have their picture done by him. Even the gargoyles. He's a legend."

"Are you sure, because I've never heard of him."

"I know this for a *fact*."

"The Green is pretty small, isn't it?"

Aggy pondered Alex's statement. "It's not. At least— I don't think it is. It can't be. If it was small, you and I would have seen each other more. Right? I've only seen you twice."

That made sense. Alex examined the photographs in the cabinet. "Does he have his picture in here some-where too? The photographer?"

"I guess so." Aggy looked upwards. The glass case stretched so high it was practically impossible to see the top.

"I wonder how old he is."

"Absolutely ancient. No one knows what he looks like anymore. He takes the pictures from behind a curtain. His son does most of the work now."

Alex peered through the glass at the various faces.

"Very disappointing though," Aggy said.

There was so many! Photographs on top of photographs. Some peeping out with just eyes, others with just mouths.

"What is?" Alex asked. The cabinet was mesmerizing. The entire history of their race was there. All you had to do was look.

"All of the pictures are taken in his studio. But *everything* is posed. See how everyone is just sitting or standing?"

She was right. All the vampires sat, or stood, next to each other. Some on stools, others on cushions. Sometimes a whole family would sit together on a large, highback couch or a divan.

"They look good to me," Alex responded.

"They do. I know. But there are no *candid* shots. He is the *most famous* vampire photographer and there are absolutely no candids." Aggy shook her head. "What a shame."

Alex was only interested in the faces. "I wonder how many are in here."

"Everyone's in there."

That didn't sound right. "You mean, all the vampires in Carpathia?"

Aggy nodded. "It's *all* of us Alex. Every single one."

Alex looked up and tried to see the top of the cabinet. Aggy was right; they were a mile high. "Aggy, I don't think it's all of us. It can't be. Besides, some people don't like their picture taken."

"*Everybody* likes their picture taken. Which means we're all in here. The humans take it to the next level though."

"What do you mean?"

"They have this way of communicating called Book-

Face." Her head shook vigorously. "I'm not kidding. They don't talk anymore. Not like you and I are talking right now I mean. They only write to each other and take pictures of themselves. They communicate on these little typewriter things that they carry in their pockets. And they *used* to go outside a really long time ago, but they don't anymore."

Alex wondered where Aggy was getting all her information. None of it sounded right.

She took a few more steps to the next glass cabinet. "But this is what I wanted to show you. Right here."

A few leaves flew in from the open windows and curled on the floor at their feet.

Alex walked up to the glass. Aggy directed his gaze to a picture among the others. It stood out against the rest. "That vampire," she said. "That's Deleter."

The vampire stood alone, with his hand curled over the back of an ornate, empty chair. His hair was slicked to the right and parted on the side. Covering his face was a mechanical apparatus, with a strange eyepiece that jutted out.

"Creepy," Aggy said. "Someone told me he doesn't look like that anymore though. It's an old picture."

"Is he a teacher?"

Her eyes popped. "Teacher? If he was, we'd be in trouble."

"Why?"

"Don't look at it anymore." Aggy pulled him away from the case. She lowered her voice to a whisper, as if, somehow, the picture just might hear her. "This is the story. He's real . . . I think. No one—and I mean *no one*, has seen him for 400 hundred years. He used to be a human."

"Human?"

"Yes. A vampire named Acacia fell in love with him and brought him to Carpathia. There's a book on it. I think Peter Picadoo wrote it."

"Where did she bring him from?"

"The human world dummy. Anyway . . . ugh. . . what then? Oh yeah. Acacia disappeared and he tried to take over. He had followers too. Mostly revenants and steampunks though. And . . . what else?" She realized her voice had begun to rise, in graduating fear. She lowered it. "He also mesmerized a number of witches who would cast spells for him."

"What is that stuff on his face?" Alex was particularly interested in the weird eye-piece that jutted out from underneath his eyebrow like a mini telescope.

The curfew bell rang.

"He was half steampunk. In the beginning I mean." Aggy glanced over her shoulder. "I don't know much about them, or the revenants. But I do know they're *all* evil. All of them. Come on."

"What happened to him?"

Aggy shook her head. "I don't know. The problem is, the author died and the book was never finished."

Alex made a mental note to check out the book from the library. "You go ahead, all right?"

"Are you sure?"

"Yeah."

"Well . . . all right. I'll stop by your wing tomorrow."

Alex watched her run off. As soon as she was gone, he went back to the cabinet. He had to look at Deleter one more time. Just one more time. He felt a link with this vampire. A bond of some sort. Deleter actually felt . . . *familiar.*

The black and white picture had faded with age, but Deleter's face had not. You could still see the black dot for an eye, (the steampunk metal was covering the other one) glaring forward, and the fingers like a claw on the edge of the chair.

A cold wind blew towards him.

And a sound of—

Footsteps?

Alex spun around. The entrance to Eventide Hall was empty. There wasn't a soul in sight.

"Hello?" Alex felt his skin prickling up. It felt like someone was there . . . watching him. Or some*thing.* "Hello?"

But there was no answer. Only a little whistle, from an open window above, and the rustling of the trees outside.

Suddenly Otis burst around the corner. "Alex! The bell!"

Alex didn't move. He was still listening. If he waited another moment, maybe he could hear what it was.

"Alex! The hall monitors! Come on!" Otis yelled. He

was jumping up and down at the end of the corridor. "They're coming!"

In the distance, vaguely, Alex could hear the flapping of little wings.

The hall monitors in which Otis was referring to were itty bitty bats. Little colored pests that flew at you the minute you were late—their tiny bat teeth snipping at your heels and yanking your hair from its roots.

"What are you doing? Come on! If they get a taste, they'll never leave you alone!"

Alex dashed—

They made it back to their corridor lickety-split, and luckily, Edwald was there holding the door open. "Run!" he shouted.

Alex could hear the bats flapping behind them, their mouths anxious for a scrumptious taste of a newbie beginner.

One of them swooped down at Otis.

"Otis, duck!" Edwald yelled.

He did. Just in time too.

The bat chomped the air and swished towards the corridor windows.

Another one zipped in front of Alex, and made a lunge at his nose.

Alex batted it away with his cape.

"Otis, cover your ears!"

He did, just as one snapped again.

Finally they reached the Walachia wing door, which Edwald was holding open, and rushed through it. The minute they cleared the entrance, Edwald threw the door shut. "That was close." He fell against the wood. "I thought the bats were going to *carry* you back."

Alex turned to Otis. "Thanks. If you hadn't come to get me I'd be bat food right now."

Otis grimaced. He was too out of breath to speak.

Klytus ran over. "So what did you guys see anyway?!"

Someone else, "Did you go to the bell tower?"

Edwald interjected, "There's supposed to be a garden over there somewhere."

Batcakes pushed in so everyone could see him. "Yeah, I heard about that. It's supposed to be huge."

And the rest of the questions came in a rush. Everyone had found at least one thing peculiar, and explanations were demanded by all.

The Walachia boys curled up on pillows, lounged in chairs, and stayed up all night by the fireplace, exchanging stories. They told each of their townships, the trees they lived in, and the caves too. And, most importantly, they told each other their dreams.

Eventually the hour grew later and later. Eyes drooped, followed by yawns, and heads lolled. Stories were told, repeated, and told again. Who knew what was going to happen, or what *could* happen.

Eventually they were all asleep on the floor, and their bed-sits forgotten.

Before drifting off, the stars glimmered at Alex through the invisible ceiling. The moon was there too. But this time it looked different. It had a face. A demented face. And from one of the eyes, a mechanical apparatus—

It was a steampunk moon!

You're dreaming . . .

You're . . . what are you?

Oh, I'm . . . falling asleep . . .

But the face looks like . . .

He could see Eventide Hall and the picture of Deleter in the cabinet. His long black cape and odd looking clothes. The watch-chain dangling from pocket to pocket.

Aggy's voice broke through the ceiling of stars.

"He's the most evil vampire of all. In the entire world!"

"There are no *completely* evil vampires. They're all good at heart."

Is that what he had said to her?

Aggy's voice grew grave. "Oh no they're not. Not him anyway. He'd kill all of us if he got the chance."

The image of her drifted away.

You're asleep Alex.

You're definitely asleep.

The moon was watching him from above. The eyepiece clicking. The mechanics turning. The mouth curling up into a weird and surreal smile.

Yes, watching him.

In the quiet.

And wondering.

14

ENEMIES

Breakfast was always brought in by Merry Molly, a Druid of much cheer, with the same darkday greeting: "Get up little creatures!" and the gentle opening of the Walachia wing door.

If you were already awake, you could hear the wheels in the hall, roll roll rolling and the caw of the dark bird singing. For in Carpathia—as you probably know by now—there is a clear division between a darkday and night. Darkday is like a human day, and night is night (as it is in the human world). Also, when a darkday approaches, so does a bright full moon. Not a normal moon, mind you, but a grand glowing light that is bright enough to see everything quite clearly.

Now Merry Molly's companion was a Brownie named Makepiece. A sour, angry little creature who absolutely, without question, completely and utterly, hated

all children.

If you haven't seen a brownie, by the way, they have wrinkled faces, elongated hands and feet, and long, upturned noses. Their ears stick out from beneath a homemade cap (which all brownies take pride in making themselves), and they have messy, chocolate colored hair.

Each morning Makepiece moved from chamber to chamber, hope hope hoping to find a beginner who had accidentally slept in. Usually he didn't find one. Everyone was too hungry by the time Molly showed up to still be asleep. *But*, every so often, he did, which would then light up his angry little face with complete and utter joy. For punishment, he would snatch up a jug of water, and dump the contents in your face. That was his favorite. Another one was screaming in your ear so you flew out of bed. The time it happened (years before) to a pixie named Puck, Makepiece yelled 'FIRE!', which sent the pixie screaming—still half asleep, don't forget—only to land in a gooey bowl of breakfast pudding. This pleased Makepiece very much, and he laughed boisterously throughout breakfast.

But Molly never noticed what Makepiece was doing, (so he was never scolded) for his brownie antics. Molly's attention was always on the food. Blood breakfast for the 'vampies', which she liked to call the vampire children, green wraps for the Druids, fruit flowers for the pixies, and wheat bread or meat for the gargoyles.

On the first darkday of school, after Molly and

Makepiece had gone, Edwald announced to all what the school term would be like. "First, you go to all the normal classes, and after lunch you go to the classes that matter."

"What are *those*?" It was Ariel who asked. He flew back into the conversation.

Edwald waved a piece of toast in the air and said, "Legends, Unique Abilities—doesn't *anyone* in here have an older brother?" His statement was meant to make everyone in the room feel stupid, and it worked.

"I do," Otis said.

Alex added, "The first half is Math, English, and Science."

Otis groaned and said, "Fun."

"The second half is what you really need to know," Edwald added as he chewed, "for the real world."

"The real world?" Batcakes asked. He was standing by the fireplace.

"When we're adultwise," Edwald responded, seriously. "And we all have to save the world." Since this was Edwald's absolute favorite statement, and most of the other boys had already heard it from him, there was no surprise from the Walachia beginners.

Suddenly the door opened and a very colorful teenage vampire stood in front of them. He wore a rich red cape that matched the color of his curly hair, and his eyes shined crystal blue.

"Beginners. I am Saber. The Organizer. Everyone keeps asking, so I will tell you right from the get-go.

You *can't* go to the school store until the last bell has rung. Got it? So don't ask me about that. It won't be open until your last class anyway. So—after I give you your class schedules, you will proceed together, *as a wing*, to the courtyard. Once there, you collect your maps. The academy is colossal. If you don't know what that means I'll tell you. It means seriously humongous. I'm not kidding. Students are always getting lost. So what I can tell you is, try to start memorizing where everything is located *now*. It will save you a lot of embarrassment later." He looked at them all very sternly. After a moment, he turned down and consulted his clipboard. "All right. First name. Edwald Trowbridge."

Edwald stepped forward.

Saber whipped the paper from the clipboard, and gave it to Edwald. "There you are. And don't be late," he added.

"I am *never* late," Edwald replied, confidently.

Saber said nothing and re-adjusted his clipboard.

The schedules were handed out quickly, and Saber said, "You have a little time before the bell rings. When it does, go to the quad." He finished with, "All right. Hopefully I'll see some of you in the field," and left.

"Field?" Batcakes asked.

Otis answered, "He means the exercise field."

Alex looked down to his class list. There, at the bottom of the page, along with the other classes, Human History was listed.

He read it again. Human History! It was the one class

he was hoping for.

Edwald addressed the group, "All right. Listen. Our most current necessity is to figure out the riddle. This classroom stuff," and he waved his paper in the air, "isn't an *adventure*. It's homework. Besides, I want us to win."

Otis turned to Edwald. "Winning isn't everything."

"Whoever told you that is a liar. Winning *is* everything," Edwald retorted.

Alex admired Otis's bravery.

"Well, it shouldn't be," Otis replied, but this time his voice was less strong, and a little unsure.

"We will win," Edwald insisted. He curled one hand into a fist and smacked it with the open palm of his other hand. "We have to. So all of us need to start thinking how we're going to solve it. We should all write it down and carry it with us. You never know when there might be a clue. Maybe in class. Or maybe just something written on some random wall. A clue could be anywhere. Anywhere!"

Edwald finished and looked at everyone for confirmation.

They looked back at him, but said nothing.

"*Well*, what do you think?"

Everyone readily agreed.

"Good, because—"

All of a sudden, the chamber door slammed open, and a group of girls entered.

Grimanesa Vex was the leader of this clan, and had already declared herself commander of the Karnstein

Wing. She stood at the top of the entryway, triumphant, with her hands on her hips, and viewed the bevy of Walachia boys with instantaneous contempt. "Well, well, well," she said.

The other girls tittered behind her.

Grimanesa had dark black hair, which fell in ringlets to her shoulders, and her face was pointed, like a hawk. She took the two short steps and moved into the room with alacrity. "I just wanted to see what it was like."

"Well, thank you for stopping by," Edwald shot back. He pushed his druid cape behind his shoulders. "But, as you can see, we are in the middle of a meeting."

Grimanesa glared at him, her eyes burning. "What did you say?"

Alex jumped forward. He could see an argument brewing. "Is it much different? From the girls dorm I mean?"

Grimanesa looked Alex up and down—from his white-haired head to his scruffy black shoes. "I wasn't speaking to you. But now that you've brought it up. Nothing is different. All the chambers are exactly the same. Exactly."

Maybe he could soothe her. "I'm Alex. This is Edwald, Otis, and—"

Grimanesa sliced the air with her hand, and cut him off. "I have decided that you are my new enemy. How do you like that?"

Alex stepped back.

"I don't think he cares," Edwald broke in, with his

arms crossed.

"He will." But she did not look back at Edwald. Instead, as though a Carpathian Queen, she turned, swept her cloak to part the sea of boys, and sauntered back to the other girls. "Let's go," she directed.

Aloof, the entourage followed her out.

"Ignore her," Edwald said.

Alex exhaled. "I don't think that'll be very easy."

Which was true, of course, and Edwald knew it. But, before he could respond, the morning bell rang with a heavy, thunderous boom.

"This is it," Alex said. And he was right. The school term had begun.

15

HUMAN HISTORY

$\mathcal{I}n$ the main courtyard, two Brownies stood on elevated stools with the Academy's school maps. Brownie Bell and Brownie Ben were happy to do the appointed task, and, unlike Makepiece, quite cheerful in the handing-out. Everyone, of course, was trying to find out where to go, by which hall, into which corridor, and by way of which courtyard (for there were many courtyards besides the main courtyard from where the Magus had stood only the night before.)

Alex and Otis approached Brownie Bell. "Here you are," she said, and both were handed school diagrams. The maps were blue and white, with tiny white dots outlining the corridors and towers, and the grounds—as well as the gardens.

Brownie Bell looked at them sternly. "This is your only copy. A second will not be issued."

"Thank you," Alex said.

Otis didn't seem to care about the map at all. "I have math first," he said, with a grunt. His face contorted before saying, "I hate math."

Alex finished his first three classes, and when the tintinnabulum rang for lunch, he dashed to the central courtyard where lunch was being set out by Merry Molly and the lunch Brownies. Otis met him—running—and stopped beneath the Crying Witch.

"Why do you think she's called that?" Otis looked up to the frozen statute. Her face was hidden by a shroud and her hands were cupped over her face to hide the tears.

"I don't know. Where do you want to sit?"

"Anywhere."

"I don't want to sit next to that girl. Whatever her name is. The crazy one who came into our wing."

"Oh yeah," Otis said. "I found out her name. Grimanesa."

Alex was looking through the crowd. Besides the beginners, there were students from all different class levels. "Do you see Edwald?"

Otis scanned the throng, but couldn't see him.

"Hi." Angelica trotted to where they stood. She

pressed her hands to the sides of her head to flatten her hair. "I've been looking for you guys. Come on, let's eat."

Otis didn't argue.

Lunch was quite scrumptious and because the tables were round, it was easy to talk to almost anyone seated. The main courtyard, Alex found out, was the central meeting place for the school, where food was served, and school dances and assemblies were usually held.

"Last night I went to the Battlement," a girl said. Alex didn't recognize her. "A thousand steps."

A dark skinned vampire boy was speaking with her. "Are you sure?"

"No. Someone just told me that. I didn't count them."

"You should have."

Angelica had finished her lunch and was using her napkin to clean up the remains on her plate. There was no real reason to do this, since the lunch brownies did the dishes, but she did it anyway. Alex watched her as she spoke to him. "I saw the gardens from the back of the school. They are sooo big. But I couldn't get through the doors to see it all. Where did you go?"

Otis interrupted, "I went to the bell tower *and* the armory."

Angelica folded her napkin onto her plate and looked at him. "What's an armory?"

Alex answered, "Armor for battle. Like when you go to war."

The answer was perplexing since there hadn't been a war for centuries. Confused, she answered, "Oh. I see."

"It was really super impose," Otis said with a huge smile.

Angelica's head cocked. "And what does *that* mean? Impose?"

"It means utterly super amazing in an IMPOSE way."

Angelica turned to Alex. "Have you heard of that? Impose? I don't think that's a real word."

Alex hadn't. "Oh sure. We say it at the Green all the time."

"The Green?"

"Where I live. My cemetery."

"Oh. Hillock Green." Angelica smacked her hands together to rid her fingers of the crumbs. "I like it. Impose."

Otis grinned.

Angelica examined him. Her deep red hair looked like a helmet framing her face. "I don't think I'll ever understand gargoyle habits. Also, your glasses are on crooked."

Otis took off his glasses and readjusted them, just as Angelica picked up her backup and stood up from the table. "I'm off. Maybe I'll see you guys after school."

After lunch, Alex got turned around while searching for his next class.

A beautiful girl stopped when she saw him. "Are you lost?"

Alex stammered, "I think so . . ." He wondered if she was a masters student.

"I'm Electra." She kneeled down. "Which class are

you looking for?"

Alex showed her his schedule and said, "Human History."

"Oh. That's a great class. It's the third door down on the left."

"Thanks."

Electra nodded and stood up. "Good luck."

"Have you ever seen one?" Alex asked. The question just popped out.

"Seen one?"

"A human. Have you ever seen one? That's what I meant."

Electra smiled and shook her head. "No," she replied, "and I hope I never do."

Alex didn't know what to say to that.

When she turned, her dress seemed to carry her down the hall. Just like a vampire angel.

Alex could feel the excitement welling up. He yelled back at her, "Thanks!", but she was already out of sight.

Aggy was in the class with him. Even though she had on a different dress, she still wore her ruby spider pendant. Also, she hadn't changed her hair. It still hung in a ponytail from the back of her head.

Alex sat down next to her.

"You made it," she said.

"Barely," Alex replied. His pushed his cape over his shoulder and looked around. "Do you see anyone else you know?"

"I don't think so."

Suddenly Alex noticed Grimanesa. She was sitting five rows up. "There's that girl."

Aggy followed Alex's gaze. "What girl?"

"Up there. Her name's Grimanesa. We're enemies."

Aggy jerked her head. "Enemies? Why?"

"I don't know. She just burst into our wing and said that I was her new enemy."

"Oh great," Aggy breezed, "she's in my wing."

Alex was about to ask her more about Grimanesa, but the professor swept in from the back of the room, down the middle aisle, and stopped at the front of the class. He had a full head of wavy, golden hair which hung in heavy strands to his shoulders. His face was strong. His arms and shoulders were huge. And though he wasn't a giant, he looked like one as he towered over the entire class. Plus, he had a magnificent blonde beard.

When he spoke, his voice was deep. "Welcome little beginners to the magical world of Human History!" It came out in a roar and with a happy bravado. His arms opened to the class. "I am Mr. Ticora."

A hand shot up from the back row.

"Yes, in the back," the professor said.

"Why do we have to learn human history? I've never even *seen* a human. And they have no magic. And no powers."

"Ahhh," replied Mr. Ticora, "but they do. And many of them have actually found it." No one knew what this meant at all. "And," he added, with a finger up in the air, "don't you—a druid—think that it is important to know the Cave Histories? Or the history of the Revenants and how they tried to overthrow the white vampires of Celtica?"

Mr. Ticora, as if casting a spell, aimed a finger at Silvanus Featherstone.

The boy jerked. Silvanus was a druid with short spikey red hair, and a wide forehead. "Ah . . . if you say so."

Everyone laughed.

"Not an answer!" he bellowed. "But, since it was funny, I forgive you. In *this* class I always want you to give your *own* opinion." He paused. "Now, do not misunderstand me, we will learn *all* histories. Of all the Carpathian peoples. But we will also learn histories of those you have yet to meet. Races that once lived. Races that are no more, and races we have yet to understand."

The beginners watched him excitedly. He was such an imposing druid, and so full of life, his enthusiasm was contagious.

"Now, can any of you tell me, possibly, why humans are important? How about you?" Mr. Ticora pointed to Aggy. "Anything . . . tell me anything at all."

"Ugh . . . maybe . . ." and a look of defeat came over her face. "No, I guess not."

"Anyone else?"

The class sat mute.

"Anyone?" he asked again.

Alex wracked his brain. For bat's sake, why couldn't he think of anything?

"You see," he said to Aggy, for her face was quite sullen. "You are not alone, and *that* is comforting."

Klytus, who sat in the third row, raised his hand. Everyone looked at him. "Everything I've read about them is about terrain wars." He paused, and since Mr. Ticora said nothing, continued, "All they do is fight. I can't think of anything they have that's important. Plus, they have this ugly orange ball that hangs in the sky."

Silvanus interjected, "My dad told me that they don't like the way they look so they are always doing things to themselves."

Alex smiled. The human debate had already started and it was only their first day of class! Of course, everything was purely conjecture. No one had ever met a human, or for that matter, seen one.

Cha Cha, a girl in the front row, twisted in her seat, and looked at Silvanus. "I read that they put lotion on themselves to get a *tan*. That's what they call it. To get darker. They don't like white skin."

The girl sitting next to her, Eloise, laughed: "That *cannot* be true."

Cha Cha gyrated her head, emphatically. "It *is* true."

"No it's not. You made that up."

"I didn't!"

Mr. Ticora smiled and stopped the tiff. "Thank you ladies. You both bring up good points." He took a long pause, "So, what I want you to think about is, what *does* a human have that is important? And since this such a difficult question, we shall have it as our mid-term exam."

The class eyeballed him.

"That means write it down," he said, and laughed.

Flurries of pencils were snapped up, notebooks flew open, and the beginners wrote down their first assignment.

But Alex didn't. That was one assignment he wasn't going to forget. Instead, he watched Professor Ticora write it on the blackboard. *What do humans have that is important?*

Alex didn't know it at the time (and how could he), that it was this teacher—the druid with the flaxen hair—that would one day save his life.

16

CAVEAT EMPTOR!

"*What'd* ya think? I was going to be a little green man at the end of a rainbow?"

Alex faltered. "I guess—"

"At least you're honest. What's your last name?"

When the last school bell chimed—to signal the end of the first darkday—the dash began. The 'dash', as it had come to be known, was the race to reach the school store.

The Academy's store was situated at the end of the main courtyard, just past a cluster of stone tables, and through two magnificently ornate wood doors. At the top of the doors, a sizable bat hung, in the typical upside down fashion. The face was pitched down, and the eyes bore into the gathering queues below. Alex couldn't tell if it was sleeping or watching. Either way, it was the largest bat he had ever seen, and probably ten tails long.

The magnificent interior held anything a student

could want or desire. Books, capes, canes, writing implements, hexes (in scrolls), magical items, and even the most tiniest of necessities, like pitch erasers—erasers which wiped away calculations in the air, so you could start from scratch. They had invisible workbooks too, so no one could steal your notes, and oddities from every region of Carpathia.

To prevent thievery, crystal webs hung from the ceiling. If any student attempted a theft, the webs would fall, and glue the culprit to the floor.

For light, gas lanterns were set throughout the store (strategically of course!), with flickering fire in their crystal spires.

Without a doubt this was the largest shop in all of Carpathia, and—some would say—even larger than the Grand Bookstore of Witchwood.

When Alex and Aggy arrived, Alex couldn't believe how many students were already at the door. The line twisted like a snake and ended at the Hall of Horrific Finds.

"We'll never get in," Aggy protested, "and I already have a test tomorrow."

But they did. Two goblins opened the main doors, and guided the students to various check-in points.

Once inside, Alex and Aggy found themselves at the head of the beginner queue.

"Name?" the leprechaun asked. He sat behind a small, lime colored desk.

"Vambarey," Alex said to the leprechaun—"Alex."

The leprechaun peered down to his stack of papers, and tapped a gnarled finger at them. He had green spectacles, which sat on an ugly nose, and Alex noticed his face was a layer cake of wrinkles. "Here's your name."

A plaque hung above the leprechaun's chair in the shape of an egg. The letters on it were gold-encrusted and read: "Caveat Emptor!"

"Excuse me? What does that mean?" Alex asked. "Ca—vee—at. Emptor."

"Fair warning to buyer!" the leprechaun proclaimed, with an arched eyebrow. He sat up from his seat, leaned forward, and pressed both hands on his table.

Alex repeated the phrase, "Fair warning to buyer."

Aggy tried to make out the meaning as well.

"Ergo," the leprechaun went on, with deadly seriousness, "it means—simply—be careful what you buy."

"Oh." Alex forced a smile. "That makes sense."

"Of course it does," and the leprechaun settled back into his chair.

Alex and Aggy exchanged furtive glances. Even though they were both short, they were definitely taller than this leprechaun, who sat perched on a chair made of wicker and—some would say—wile.

The leprechaun consulted his chart. "It looks like you have good credit. Not great, mind you, but *good*. Tell them your last name at the register with your purchases."

A pixie dashed through the air and hovered beside Goldbomb (which was the leprechaun's name), hands out and waiting.

The leprechaun circled a number on the topmost slip, which was Alex's credit, and lifted the paper into the air. "We are most efficient here," he said.

The pixie snatched it from him, and zipped off.

"Well, move aside now boy. Let the girl in."

Aggy stepped forward nervously and said, "Agatha."

"Looks like you're a vampire too." Goldbomb yanked her credit slip from the top of the stack. "Come closer please." The leprechaun gave her the once over, and looked past her to the line of gathering students. "I don't know where the druids are anymore. The school used to be filled with them and now we just get vampire after vampire." The statement came out in a huff of disappointment. "Well, anyway, what's your last name?"

"Durkin," she said.

The leprechaun followed the same bit, but told Aggy she had *less than great* credit, and finished with checking off her name.

"Now both of you," he scolded, "knock off. You act like you've never been here before!"

Alex was about to tell the leprechaun that, actually, they hadn't, but before he could say anything, the leprechaun became much vexed, and started screaming that everyone needed to *PROGRESS*. "Much, much faster!" he yelled out. "Otherwise, everyone will miss dinner!"

Somewhere in the back, a gargoyle groaned.

Alex lowered his voice as they walked away. "I think he's a little moody."

Aggy agreed.

Alex already knew his direction. He immediately pushed through the throngs, past the crowded check stands, and to a neon sign buzzing above an entryway marked *Textbooks*.

"That's modern," Alex told Aggy, and indicated the sign. He stopped under it.

"Modern?"

"Humans made it up," Alex added.

"I think it's called neon," Aggy said.

A flush of capes (with students attached) rushed from the textbook chamber opening and almost blasted them off their feet.

Luckily, Aggy was quick-witted, and pulled Alex aside before they were plodded.

The first thing Alex noticed about the book cases, which made up the aisles themselves, was they were all crooked. They curved up, like winding streets, and each bookcase inter-locked like a giant wavy puzzle. Along each aisle, and next to these snake-like shelves, a tall ladder stretched up, and was secured at the top. Obviously so you wouldn't topple. Also, the ladder could roll from one end to the other, which helped.

A girl named Isla ran up to them. She grabbed Aggy's arm. "There you are. Come on. Our wing's buying stuff together." Her eyes flickered to Alex, for an instant, before she said, "You don't mind, do you?"

He was about to say 'no', but—

"Good," and the girl yanked Aggy in the opposite direction.

Aggy looked back to Alex with a flush of embarrassment. "I'll see you later—"

"Bye—"

"We found the first clue," Isla whispered. She had already forgotten that Alex was even alive. "Well, I think we did. Well, Magan thinks she did. It's a good idea for sure. Pretty good. Not great. But pretty good. And no one else has come up with anything, so why not investigate it, right? That's what I was thinking. And I certainly haven't come up with anything. Believe me, I wish I had. I really do. But I haven't. Not one thing. Zippo!"

Alex didn't hear the rest, but he did find the history section, quite easily, which was right next to the vampire accessories aisle, ninth row from the front.

Alex wrestled his notebook from his backpack and consulted his scrawl. *Melinger's Math 1, Composition, A Carpathian Start*, and *Humans 101.*

The human books were at the top.

Alex ascended the ladder, which didn't seem too safe, and halted a few rungs from the highest point. He had never been afraid of heights, thanks to a copious amount of tree climbing back at the Green, and now he was thankful for those carefree summers.

Volumes and volumes sat there, waiting to be found, and with the most curious inscriptions he had ever seen. *The Wizard of Oz, Scottish History, Frankenstein*—that sounded good!—and all sorts of other strange books, oddly titled.

Alex climbed higher.

The 8th shelf up had even more: *The Earth and Carpathian Divide*, *The Revenant Revolt*, and *The History of Vampires in the Moving Picture Show*.

"Did you find it?"

Alex looked down, surprised. At the base of the ladder, all of his Human History classmates were clustered, even Grimanesa.

Silvanus Featherstone stood on the bottom rung, anxiously gripping the ladder. "Throw the copies to me and I'll hand them out. It's easier."

"I haven't found them yet." The ladder wobbled and Alex gripped it a little tighter.

"Go higher," Silvanus suggested. "Maybe they're on the top shelf."

Alex did so, and sure enough, like Silvanus had said, the course books were there. Stacked together neatly. "They're here."

"Toss 'em to me," Silvanus said.

Alex took one from the stack. It took two hands to hold it. "It's heavy. Wow."

"Don't worry about it," Silvanus said, "I can catch anything." Which was an understatement since Silvanus Featherstone was destined to be one of the most famous ball players in all of Carpathia—if not the most famous. His father had given him a dark ball for Halloween the year before, and now he carried it with him wherever he went. Currently, it was hidden in his back pocket.

Alex dropped the book to Silvanus, who caught it easily.

"I hope this is for all four years," Silvanus muttered.

"Why?" a boy asked from the back.

"Because this book is one thousand pages long!"

Alex turned to the shelf again. He pushed another book aside to reveal a different stack. "Silvanus?"

Silvanus looked up. "Yeah?"

"I don't think so."

"What do you mean?" Silvanus asked.

Alex peered over his shoulder and down to his anxious classmates, "Because there's a book up here called Humans: Year 2."

Silvanus rolled his eyes. "Oh great." He turned to the girl beside him and handed her the book. "Here," he said, sarcastically, "enjoy."

"Thanks a lot," the girl answered. Her name was Florencia. She had kinky hair with beads in it. She glared at the group and said, with equal sarcasm, "Let's all read about people we're never going to meet in our entire life."

Alex laughed.

It was most definitely, unequivocally, and without a doubt, going to be a mind-blowing, bat flapping, witch cackling, awe-inspiring year.

17

LALLAR

Otis and Alex had finally reached the front of the checkout line.

The cashier was an old, potbellied, female goblin. She wore a furry scarf and a huge string of pearls, which offset her bulbous neck. The scarf, of course, looked utterly ridiculous, as well as the pearls, but she thought otherwise. Mid-check out she halted, abruptly, and adjusted her jewelry. First the hoop earrings, followed by the bracelets, next the scarf, and lastly the pearls. No wonder the lines were taking so long. After the primping, she went back to Otis's purchases. "You can't have that."

The woman—if you could call her a woman—snatched one of Otis's Solopso sticks and set it beside her register. Alex wondered if she was going to eat it later.

"Why not!?" Otis exclaimed.

The goblin acted oblivious and plucked something else from his pile. "Nor this!"

Otis had gathered up a variety of candies, none of which he could get back at home, and added them to his school books.

Alex wanted to help, but didn't know what to do.

The goblin continued, "What else have we got? Oh—lookeee here. Another one." Her big hand plucked out a gold-wrapped ball. She smiled wickedly and dangled it in front of Otis's mouth. "These are delicious! I always love them for a snack." She waited as long as she could, for torture's sake, and then tossed it over her shoulder. The gold ball thudded in the go-back pile behind her. "What a shame."

Alex piped up, "The leprechaun said his credit was fine and he could get what he wanted."

Harriet—that was the name of this thing—smacked a finger on one of the register keys. A ding rang out. "That's what he said, is it? You sure about that?"

The answer was no, but Alex went ahead anyway. "Yes. I'm sure. That's what he said."

"Alex, it's all right. I don't need that stuff." Otis mumbled the statement while staring at the floor.

Goblin Harriet, without looking at either of them, adjusted her pearls again. "Don't you know what candy and sweets *do* to gargoyles? Hmmmm? You probably haven't read about that in your vampire books, have you?"

"Ugh . . ." Alex looked around. Everyone was starting to stare. "Ugh . . . no."

"Ohhhhh. I see. Well, my boy, candy makes gargoyles most unagreeable. That is if they don't eat it with rockweed. I guess you didn't tell him *that* did you? Convenient." The goblin glared triumphantly. "Maybe you should read *Gargoyles 101* instead of that book about humans you have there."

"I don't need it. Really," Otis said again, weakly.

"I know you don't neeeeed it, but you want it, don't you?" she drawled, her voice oozing.

Alex wanted to bop her upside the head.

Suddenly, she stood up. Her lumpy body had been squished between the table and the cash register platform.

"GOLDBOMB!" she screamed.

Everybody froze. Heads turned.

The cash registers halted.

"GOLDBOMB! This GARGOYLE says he has CREDIT for CANDY!"

Alex watched in horror as every eye in the store shot in their direction.

Otis smacked his claws to the top of his head. "Oh, hells bells!"

The minute Otis said it, Harriet gasped. Her hands flew to her chest like an innocent maiden.

The leprechaun, from the other side of the store, hoisted himself onto his table, which brought him to full height with the beginners, and screamed back: "WHICH ONE!?"

When the goblin started talking again, she was all business. Alex realized that her 'shock' at Otis's outburst was as fake as the chipped pearls that hung around her neck.

"THIS ONE. RIGHT IN FRONT OF ME. LAST NAME—" She checked the credit slip at the top of the register. "FALLSTREAK. FIRST NAME—OTIS."

The leprechaun shook his papers in the air angrily from his perch. "ARE YOU KIDDING!? LOOK AT THIS LINE!"

"HE *SAYS* HE HAS A CREDIT! FOR CANDY."

Harriet held her head up, her lipstick-painted goblin lips all pushed-out, while one hand caressed her necklace in reverence.

Otis turned red.

Alex knew he had to do something. Otherwise, Otis would never live this down. "He doesn't care about it!"

High falutin Harriet pretended not to notice. "Well, we have to check now, don't we? After all, it is CANNNDDDY."

Otis pulled Alex's cape, "Alex, let's go."

But Alex knew they had to stay. If they didn't, they'd be a laughing stock. "Otis, no."

Goldbomb crawled down from the desk, grabbed a different stack of papers, and started going through them. "You all have to wait now," he said.

A loud groan reverberated through the line.

"I have to find this Otis!" he yelled out, his green face actually turning scarlet.

Harriet smiled and fluffed her scarf.

Alex didn't want to look back. The line behind them

was getting bigger, and not just with beginners, but all class levels, which made it even worse.

"Let the kid have some candy!" a voice shouted, from somewhere.

Harriet took no notice of the comment.

Goldbomb found Otis's name card. He crawled up and stood on his desk again. "FOUND IT!" he yelled. "NO CREDIT FOR CANDY!"

"JUST WHAT I THOUGHT!" Harriet shrilled. Suddenly she was frazzled and annoyed. After squeezing back into her seat, she peered down to Otis, triumphantly, and arched her eyebrow. That is, if you could call it an eyebrow. "Do you have anything else in that pile?"

"No!" Otis shouted. His face was redder than a tomato.

"Good," she retorted, and finished ringing him up. "Next!"

Both boys walked back to the Walachia wing in silence. Alex wasn't sure how to break the ice.

"I've never been so embarrassed in all my life," Otis finally said. "Am I still red?"

Alex looked at his friend's face. "No. You're good."

"And absolutely everyone had to be there. I really don't like that woman."

Alex nodded. "Next time make sure you know what your credit is for."

"I knew," Otis exasperated. He shifted the rope satchel to his other shoulder. "I just didn't know that *she* did."

"Maybe we should call her scary Harriet."

Otis laughed. "Or Hag Harriet."

"Yes! Waaayyy better."

Otis shifted his books from one arm to the other. "I hope she's doesn't work there full time."

"She probably does," Alex countered. "She's the type that never misses a day of work."

Otis shook his head. "I'll never eat candy again."

"Hey kid!" A voice echoed through the corridor behind them.

Alex and Otis swung around.

About twenty feet away stood the masters student, Lallar. A black gargoyle of the Shadow Caves. Male, with white spiked horns on his head, muscles everywhere, and wings in the middle of his back. He had no hair at all, and to Alex, he looked like a perfect statue. Well, a statue that lifted lots of weights anyway! His black skin reminded Alex of the night sky. Rich and shiny. In his right hand he held two books. But in his left—

"Catch!" Lallar yelled out, and tossed something through the air.

Otis caught the object with one hand. It was one of the candies that Harriet had confiscated—the glistening gold ball of pure chocolate.

"Thanks!" Otis exclaimed.

Lallar nodded, and smiled. His teeth were so white, they actually shimmered. "Don't eat it with rockweed," he said. Alex could hear the sarcasm in his voice.

"I won't!" Otis shot back, his face brimming with a gargantuan grin. "Wow!"

Lallar tipped his head again, turned, and disappeared.

Alex had never seen a teenage gargoyle before. "Is that what you're going to look like when you're older?" he asked.

Otis stared into the empty hallway. "Boy," he answered, agog, "I hope so."

18

THE FIRST CLUE

"*What* do you think it means?" Otis asked. His spectacles were dangling at the end of his nose. He pushed them up.

"Alex, read it again," Edwald said.

The fire blazed in the first chamber of the Walachia Wing, and all the boys had gathered together, to hear—again—the Magus Challenge.

"All right. Here it goes," Alex said. He read it:

> *In the Night Gallery*
> *of the voivode,*
> *A clever woman sits.*
> *Beside her might be*
> *the key to all,*

But if not,
then why not quit?

There, where the wind blows hot and fierce,
A single flower grows.
Protected by a king,
Of the Ozymandias ring,
The dead red river flows.

Bring it back and win the prize,
But is it worth the price?
It helps all little ones to be,
Healthy, happy, alive—and free.

Alex finished and folded the paper neatly. He had jotted the riddle down between classes and now always carried it in his pocket.

Batcakes stepped forward triumphantly and said, "I have no idea what that means," and then slumped down into the largest chair.

Edwald scolded him. "Well you have to *think*! Don't give up so easily."

Batcakes shrugged.

Otis threw his large arms into the air. "If we just had the *first* part!"

"Well, Edwald, you're the genius," Batcakes finally answered, "What do you think it means?"

"I'm not a genius," Edwald said, with much emphasis, "but I want to be."

"I think the little ones are the pixie race," Ariel said. "But we have no broken tree."

Alex turned to Otis. "What's your take on it?"

Otis was about to answer, but before he could, a voice rang out from the other side of the wing.

"He isn't going to know *anything*. He's a gargoyle. All they do is fly around castle tops."

A few feet away, Grimanesa Vex stood saucily in the doorway, with the Karnstein girls huddled behind her.

Roused, Edwald blasted, "Don't you ever knock?!"

She threw her head back in response and went on with, "Trying to figure out the riddle?" as she walked down the steps. "We've already figured out the first part. Haven't we?" The girls behind her nodded in agreement.

Alex saw Aggy in the back of the gaggle. Their eyes met.

Grimanesa caught the exchange, and shifted her focus to Alex. "What are *you* looking at?"

"Nothing," Alex snapped. "If you know so much, who is the clever woman?"

Grimanesa huffed. "As if I would tell you. We're enemies."

Edwald rolled his eyes. "Why don't you get out of here. Don't you have better things to do than try to get the answer from us?"

"That's a laugh," she snooted.

"Is it?" Edwald moved up to her. "If you think you are going to get that prize over us, you're crazy. Clearly, you don't have a gargoyle in your wing. Or a pixie."

"Who needs gargoyles and pixies? Everyone knows that anything flying through the air has absolutely no mind for puzzles, riddles, or math."

"Really? Otis happens to be the best mathematician in his clan. So I guess that makes you wrong then."

"Oh pleeeeaasee," she drawled.

Otis stood with his back to the fireplace—in shock—staring—with one large claw on each cheek.

Grimanesa glanced at him and snickered. "Mathematician. That's a good one."

"It's true," Alex said, defensively.

"Well, we have an elemental," she fired, "how about that?"

"So do we," Edwald retorted.

This took her by surprise. She looked around. "Who?"

Everyone froze. Total silence.

"I thought so." Grimanesa turned and flounced up the small flight of stairs to the other girls. "Let's go," she demanded. She turned back to Edwald, who she now concluded was the leader of the Walachia boys, and said, "You're going to lose. You don't have what it takes to win."

Edwald jumped forward. "Yes we do!" His voice was almost a screech.

Alex questioned her, "What makes you think that?"

Grimanesa smiled, sweetly. "Because anything worth

having means that someone is compromised."

"I guess that's going to be you," Edwald retorted.

Grimanesa flicked her fingers at him. "We'll see, won't we?"

One of the girls swung open the Walachia wing door.

With that, Grimanesa turned, flipped her cape, and flounced back into the corridor.

The rest of the tittering clan trailed behind.

Tori Tune, who was always given the unhappy task of cleaning up, shrugged nervously (as if to say, *I'm so, so sorry*), and gently shut the door.

After a moment, Otis said, "I'm terrible at math," and a few of the boys laughed.

Edwald looked frazzled. "She just came over here to find out if we know anything."

"And now she knows we don't," Cian replied, from the other side of the chamber. This was the boy elemental, who emerged meekly from the back, and commented quietly.

"Let's just forget about her and try to figure it out," Alex insisted.

Edwald nodded.

"I know one thing," Alex went on, "The Night Gallery is in the school. It has to be."

"Are you sure?" Batcakes asked.

"No," Alex answered. "But—it's a good guess. I doubt they would have us leaving the grounds to try and figure out the riddle."

Edwald moved over to Alex. "I completely agree."

Unexpectedly, a gentle rap echoed up from the Walachia wing door.

The boys turned.

Edwald dashed to it, ready for another confrontation. When he threw it open, Aggy stood in the door frame, alone. "Is Alex here?"

Edwald glared at her. "Maybe."

Alex reached the door. "Aggy?"

"Hi. Sorry about . . . " Aggy glanced over her shoulder. The hallway behind her was empty.

"You don't have to apologize for her," Alex said.

"Someone should," Edwald spouted, "that girl needs serious help."

"Well," Aggy replied, softly, "she is a little pushy."

"A little!" Edwald exclaimed, cheekily.

Ariel flew to the door and hovered over them, his wings buzzing.

Aggy noticed the pixie, but pressured for time lest she be caught, directed her attention to Alex. "I just came to say that . . . if you need to find something, you and I have already been there."

"We have?" Alex thought for a second. They had? *Pop!* It came to him. "We have! Right!" Alex was thrilled. "I'll see you tomorrow at lunch."

She nodded, looked at all the boys one more time, and then vanished into the hall.

Edwald was about to close the door, but hesitated. "What's her name again?" he asked.

"Aggy," Alex told him. He walked down the steps to

the center of the chamber.

The Walachia boys blurted "What did she say?" "Can it help us?", and, "Maybe she's trying to trick you?", and more questions of that sort.

"She's not," Alex said firmly, "and now I know where the Night Gallery is."

A burst of instantaneous clapping erupted throughout the wing.

"Pretty sure," Alex emphasized, "not a hundred percent."

Edwald clapped his hands. "99 percent is good by me! Let's go."

"We're going to need something else though."

"What?" Ariel yipped.

Alex ran back to his bed-sit. It only took a second before he was pushing back the dividing curtain and running back to them.

Everyone waited in anticipation.

Alex reached them and held the book in the air. "The Vampedia," he proclaimed.

Ariel zipped over and touched it.

"Bring it! Lets go!" Edwald hurrahed. He rushed to grab his cape.

"This is too easy," Pennybrown voiced. He ran his fingers through his spiky hair. "I have a feeling we're going to spend the entire year trying to figure this thing out."

"Probably," Alex said. "But it doesn't hurt to be the early bat."

Pennybrown looked at him. "Early bat?"

"The early bat gets the mosquitoes."

Pennybrown corrected him, "You mean the early bird gets the worms. That's the phrase."

Alex was about to protest—

"You guys!" Otis yelled. He smacked his claws together. "Let's go!"

In one wave, all the Walachian boys rushed out and bounded into the hall.

The first clue was theirs! And they were about to find it. The place that they had all heard about, but had never seen—the Night Gallery.

19

IN THE FLOOR?

A month later, the Night Gallery was still a mystery. Of course all the students hounded their teachers, but no one would say a peep.

"Can we have a clue if we do an extra assignment?"

Nope! Not even a hint my little one! Carpathia knows how to keep its secrets.

That night the boys searched Eventide Hall, as Aggy had suggested, but found nothing. After that, they searched the library. (Well, as much as it could be searched anyway—it was too large to look everywhere.) Nothing was found.

"I thought you said it was in the hall?" Alex asked Aggy later.

"It is," she whispered.

"Where in the hall?"

"I don't know. I just know it's in there. Somewhere."

Perhaps it was a picture or a drawing in a book? These ideas were suggested, and more and more books were searched, but still, nothing had been found in Eventide Hall. Alex told his fellow wingmates that the Night Gallery was a secret hall of ancient vampire paintings. And even though it came as an actual fact—directly from the Vampedia—no one could prove it.

"Yes, but we don't know for sure! Maybe the encyclopedia is wrong. You never know."

No, you never did.

Aggy and Alex had become good friends, but in the matter of the competition, they said nothing.

At night, Alex stared up at the stars through the invisible ceiling of the Walachia wing, and wondered about his parents. About Hillock Green too. He missed his father reading him stories and his mother tucking him in. "Shall I close your coffin lid?" every night she would ask, and he would nod, and smile. It all seemed so distant now. Like a far away dream.

The next darkday, after math class, Alex found himself in Eventide Hall—again. He went to the picture of Deleter and peered at it. How many times had he looked at that face? So many, he couldn't even count.

Two girls were at the end of the corridor, examining the floor.

"You don't need a note pad to look for the Night Gallery," one of them said.

"I know. I just thought if I found a clue . . . "

"I have been here a million times. Trust me, there

is *nothing* here. Nothing. And there is nothing in these floors either. I know everything there is to know about stone walls, stone floors, and stone houses. No one knows more about it than I do. No one!" The girl's hands were situated on her hips and she was staring at the girl across from her. Alex recognized her from one of his classes. Her name was Miranda Olefin. "And I also know all about carpet too," she uttered. Miranda was round, like a swollen pink grapefruit, and her carrot orange hair twisted on top of her head in a mess of rubber bands. Black rimmed glasses sat at the end of her stout nose. "Like I said, if there was something in these floors I would know about it. I know everything there is to know about that!" she kept saying. "Everything!"

Alex turned back to the photograph of Deleter. Except . . . there was something wrong.

It couldn't be. Wait—

A strange wind blew in from one of the open windows.

Impossible!

But—

Deleter's hand was now by his leg! It was not curled on the chair like before, but hanging, and flat. The hand had moved! And there was something else too. The face was different. Darker. Stranger.

Otis dashed into the corridor. He bounded to Alex and blurted out, breathlessly, "Edwald knows where the Night Gallery is!"

Alex kept his eyes on the photograph. "He says that

all the time Otis."

"This time he says he knows for sure."

Maybe he was wrong? The picture couldn't have changed.

"What do you think?" Otis asked. His face was flushed scarlet.

Alex turned to his friend. "He's wishing."

Otis nodded in defeat. "I know."

"Then why are you so excited?"

Otis shrugged. "I guess I was just hoping."

Alex turned back to the picture. Deleter's hand was still by his leg, as if it had always been there.

"What is it?" Otis asked. He followed Alex's gaze to the cabinet.

"Nothing. I thought I saw something."

"Really?"

"I thought I did." Alex shook it off. "Come on. Let's go eat."

"Dinner!" The word exploded from Otis's mouth. "Now I'm happy."

As they walked back, Alex thought of Deleter and the empty chair. The hand had moved, there was no doubt about that. But in Carpathia, moving photographs weren't so unusual. It was an old trick to spook someone. Everyone did it at Halloween.

That's what it is. It's just a spook picture. Nothing more than that. Just a spook.

Alex changed gears. "Maybe he does know where it is this time."

"I hope," Otis said, but his mind was already on potatoes, vegetables, porridge—and, most of all, candy. Of course Otis wanted to solve the riddle as much as anyone, but not at the cost of missing a meal.

The night wind whistled through the windows and Alex noticed a few monitor bats sitting on the sills.

"Have you ever heard of a vampire named Deleter?" Alex asked.

"Sure. He's the demon vampire."

Alex was surprised. "You've heard of him?"

"Sure. My dad used to scare us by telling us that the demon vampire would eat us if we didn't eat all our potatoes."

"Really?"

"After that I looked it up and found out that vampires don't eat people. They get all their food from the blood trees, and plants. I never told him though."

"Smart."

"Sometimes I get good ideas," Otis replied. "But he still says it whenever we have potatoes. Why do you ask?"

Alex wondered how much he should tell his friend. "No reason," he said.

"But he is real. I know that. And no one knows if he is alive or dead. Or undead." Otis thought the 'undead' part was funny, and laughed. "Do you think he's alive?"

"Well . . . I think you should always eat your potatoes."

Otis stopped laughing.

They had both reached the Walachia wing corridor.

"I should?" Otis asked, frightened.

Alex nodded. "But not because of him. Mostly because they're just really, really good."

Otis smiled. "That's for sure!"

Alex knew that when considering a gargoyle's stomach, little white lies were best.

20

PRECIOUS

That night, Alex went to his bed-sit early. He took off his cape, hung it on its wooden peg, and crawled into his coffin. There were so many things dancing in his mind. The riddle that no one could figure out. Deleter. The strange history of the humans.

Mr. Ticora had given an assignment which everyone was required to read out loud to the class, and it was due in a few darkdays.

Alex couldn't wait to tell everyone what he had found. His presentation was called '*Human Monsters*'. Evidently, humans kept behemoths in large caves called 'garages'. The beast had a see-through head and the humans sat inside it. Like a train, it took them all sorts of places. They also screamed like dragons, these creatures, and needed to drink buckets of a food called 'gas'. They could talk back too, and, the weirdest part of all—they sang! All sorts of different ditties as long as you knew how to push the right 'button', which Alex figured was like scratching the head of bat, or maybe petting a hound. If only he could find a drawing of the beasties, everything would be perfect!

"Alex, wake up."

Alex looked up. Otis was standing over him. "I'm not asleep."

"Come on."

"Where? What's going on?"

"Trust me. Come on."

Alex crawled out of his coffin. He grabbed his cape. "What is it?"

Alex followed Otis to the Walachia wing reading room.

"Otis, close the door," Edwald demanded.

Otis did.

Edwald walked further into the reading alcove, and peaked into each cubby. All the old fluffy cushions sat empty, and the couches too. Everyone was asleep.

"Good." Edwald walked back and stopped in front of them. "There's no time for sleeping. See this?" He pulled out a small purple bottle from his pocket and held it up. "We have to drink it."

"What happened to you at dinner?" Alex asked. "I kept looking for you. Otis said that you—"

"Never mind that," Edwald said hurriedly. "We all have to drink this."

Alex squinted to get a better view of the vial. The

reading room was filled with shadows. "What is it?"

Edwald didn't wait. He unscrewed the cap, lifted the bottle to his lips, and took a gulp.

Otis and Alex watched in suspense.

Nothing happened.

Edwald handed the bottle to Alex. "Drink," he said.

Alex held the bottle up to the light. "But what is it?" Whatever was inside had a slight green glow to it. "You know vampires can't just drink anything, right?"

"Of course I do! It is 100% vampire drinkable!"

"All right," Alex said, and took a whiff first. He lifted the bottle to his lips, "Bats up."

But instead of a nice chocolate milk (vampire chocolate milk that is!), the drink seemed to go down in chunks and stay there. "Blah!"

"Come on." Edwald crossed his arms. "It's not that bad."

"It doesn't taste good?" Otis's face collapsed.

Alex held out the bottle. "Sure. If you like rotted pumpkins and mud."

Edwald plucked the bottle from Alex's hand and gave it to Otis. "He's exaggerating. Besides, you like rotted pumpkins and mud."

"No I don't. I've tasted mud and—"

"Well just pretend you do," Edwald demanded. "It's a silence potion. And if there's anyone in this wing that needs to be silent, it's *you*."

Otis examined the vial between two clawed fingers. "How long does it last?"

"Long enough for us to find the first clue."

Alex puzzled over the vial's source. "Where did you get it from?"

"That witch girl Eloise. Actually, she's a vampire, but I think she fancies herself a witch. Anyway, she made it for us."

Alex looked at Edwald. "Why would she do that?"

"I had to tell her the clue about Eventide."

"What?!" Alex couldn't believe Edwald gave away the only clue they had so far.

Edwald defended himself: "It doesn't matter! So what if she knows. We're stuck and no one can get to the next level. If someone doesn't get to the next level, no one is going to win." Which was impossible to argue since it was the truth. "I took a risk." Edwald pushed the drink closer to Otis's mouth. "Now come on. *Drink*."

"What's in it though?" Gargoyles don't eat anything without knowing *all* of the contents, which is why most of the greatest chefs are gargoyles.

"Berries," Edwald voiced. But when he said it, he looked at Alex and shook his 'no'.

"Gargoyles are brave," Otis announced, out of the clear blue, and swallowed the contents in one mighty gulp.

Edwald and Alex watched.

"Well?" Alex asked.

Otis held up the bottle. "It's not berries," he told them, as if they didn't already know. "It's not that bad I guess."

"You're crazy," Alex blurted out. "That was the worse

thing I've ever tasted."

Edwald took the vial from Otis's claw. "Forget about all that. Let's *go*."

The adventurers hustled out of the Walachia Wing, down the corridor, and towards Eventide Hall. Otis was jumping happily. Finally! He could be as loud as he wanted! He could even scream if he wanted to! And NO ONE would tell him to keep his voice down.

"Hey!" Edwald whispered harshly. He waved his hand at Otis. "Just because they can't *hear* you, doesn't mean they can't *see* you. It's not an invisibility potion."

Otis stopped leaping. "Oh. Right. Sorry."

"And we have to be careful of the monitors too. If they see us they'll chase us back to the wing."

After a few more turns they reached Eventide Hall, which, incidentally, led to the History department's main corridor.

"Over there," Edwald said. "See it?"

At the end of the corridor, a miniature door stood between two much larger doors.

"What do you mean? The janitor's door?" Alex asked.

"Yeah, that's it."

Otis looked at it skeptically. "Are you sure?"

"I'm telling you, that's it," Edwald insisted.

Alex remembered the first time he had seen a janitor. (In Carpathia, all janitors were hobgoblins.) The creature had insisted Alex remove himself from his seat. The little thing was covered in hair, had a wide nose, and stood 2 feet tall. It held a broom in one hand and a dustpan in the other.

"I don't think the seat is dirty," Alex had said at the time. He was trying to study for a math test and the beastie kept poking him with the end of a broom.

"Much dirt," the hobgoblin said, "see," and the receptacle was held up for inspection.

Alex looked at it.

"See," the hobgoblin said again.

The pan was completely empty.

"All right, I'll move. Just give me a second."

The answer pleased the creature very much, and after sweeping the area, the hobgoblin shook the dustpan into a large pouch, which hung from its belt, and trotted off.

Between classes, the stubby creatures sang. Little ditties they hummed in unison while gathering dirt. If one began, the rest would chime in, and so forth.

Everyday the janitors scuttled through the corridors, but no one ever paid any attention. They were as common as fireflies.

Now Edwald was suggesting this might be *the key to all, or why not quit,* because of the sheer improbability.

The door that faced them was only two and a half feet high, with narrow sides.

"It's so obvious, that's why no one has thought of it," was Edwald's logic.

"I think it's the best idea you've had," Otis said.

Edwald beamed at the compliment.

"All right," Alex plotted, "what next? How do we get in? I've seen them lock the doors at night. And they only come out at darkday."

Otis tapped his chin.

"I've already thought of that." Edwald pulled a key from his jacket pocket. "A gift from Ariel."

"Berry cool!" Otis grabbed the key. "Why didn't he come with us?"

"He wouldn't say," Edwald replied, and then snatched the key back out of Otis's hand. "Your hands are too big. I'll have to do it."

Alex viewed their surroundings. "I hope this silence potion doesn't wear off."

Edwald tossed his head dramatically. "You're such a worry wart. Come on."

The boys ran to the door.

Edwald kneeled down first, inserted the key, and gave it a little turn to the right. The lock clicked, and the door opened.

Edwald glanced over his shoulder. "It worked. I'll go first."

The three beginners crouched, single file, and crawled through the hobgoblin entrance.

"I'll bet every dirty disgusting thing is kept in these rooms. Old gum and shoe goo for sure," Otis complained. "And snot too."

Alex grimaced.

"I thought gargoyles didn't mind dirt," Edwald said, without looking back.

"No," Otis said, firmly, "gargoyles do *not* like dirt."

Alex made a mental note to look up gargoyles in the

school library. So far, everything he had read about them had been *totally* wrong. Plus, he still didn't understand what Harriet meant about gargoyles not eating candy. Just how disagreeable could a gargoyle get, anyway?

Alex remembered a human phrase—he had read it in Chapter 52 of his Humans book—'*don't judge a book by its cover*'. Humans must be a clever sort, he thought, they had all sorts of funny sayings.

"This is it," Edwald said, and scooted through the doorless opening at the end of the tunnel. He stood up and brushed off his pants and cape.

Alex and Otis followed suit.

A long chamber stretched out before them, filled with rectangular tables.

"What are those things?" Otis asked.

The walls were lined from floor to ceiling with shelves, and on each shelf, containers sat one after the other.

"They're jars I think," Edwald said. "They look like glass jars."

Alex tried to use his vampire vision again—nothing. He wondered how old you had to be for it to start working. "Why are there so many?" he asked.

"They're filled," Otis said, "with something . . ."

Alex stared at the shelves. "That is *really* weird."

Otis patted his head to get the little grey cells working. "It looks like they're all filled with the same stuff."

To the Carpathian Academy janitors, the contents were most precious. Not to mention, an absolute secret.

Of course the janitors knew that with the proper key, or even scroll, their little rooms could easily be discovered. With that being the case, and after profuse pleading with the Magus for *much much needed* protection—guards were procured, and placed as defenders.

Luckily, the boys were only going to run into *one* of the fiends . . . But, as the saying goes—sometimes one is enough.

21

HOBGOBS

Alex went to the closest shelf and withdrew one of the jars. "They're heavy."

Otis stepped forward, adjusted his glasses, and tried to inspect the contents. Alex held it up for him. "Nothing's moving," he deduced.

Alex shook it. "I think . . ." and he peered through the shiny, see-through glass and said, "I think it's . . . dirt."

"Dirt?" Edwald walked over to them.

"Yes." Alex joggled the container some more, then said with finality, "dirt."

"The little buggers," Edwald chuckled. "They're collecting all the dirt in the school. They're bringing it back here and putting it in all these jars."

The three of them contemplated the situation.

"But why?" Alex put out, "What for?"

Edwald shrugged. "Who knows?"

Otis tapped the glass. "What does the label say?"

The label was crisp and clean. Alex leaned in and read it. "Science."

"Must be dirt from the Science Department," Edwald said. "Those dirty little hobgobs."

Which was a funny phrase, since they were far from dirty.

"Shssshh," Otis said.

"Otis. No one can hear us."

"Oh. Yeah. I knew that."

Alex asked them again, "But whyyy? There must be some reason." He turned the container around in his hands and shook it again. The dirt sifted from side to side.

"They're hobgobs," was all Edwald could say, as if that was enough to explain the whole random event.

From that night forward, all the janitors in the school were nick-named hobgobs. Somehow the word became quite popular, and later—many many many years later, in the new edition of the *Vampedia*, *Volume 382*, the slang term was recorded, and documented, and Edwald the Eldest, Druid of the Drooping Forest, was properly credited with the impromptu creation.

"You guys—look at this." Otis stood next to a large gold scale. The contraption stood on one of the wooden tables halfway into the room. "They're weighing it too."

Alex and Edwald ran to him.

"See." Otis pointed to the pile on the weighing machine.

"They're collecting it and weighing it," Alex said.

Otis pushed the scale. It swung back and forth. "We wouldn't need hobgobs in our cave. My mom keeps it so clean you can barely sit on a rock."

Edwald was already on to the next item of business. "Come on. Let's search everything—"

Without warning, one of the dirt defenders rushed out of an adjacent room, and halted in front of them.

The boys froze.

The creature's tiny black face was scrunched, with folds of skin around its marble eyes, and the lower lip pushed out below a single tooth. Beige fur covered the stout, fat body, and on the domed head, two small metal stubs protruded inside a set of floppy ears.

Otis stepped back, terrified. "It's a hideous creature."

The guardian sprung forward, and tipped its head. *Friend or foe?* it appeared to be asking, but no words came out.

"It's a pugenstein," Alex said happily. He snapped his fingers to try to bring the beast closer. "Come on, come on."

Edwald watched Alex try to befriend the dog. "Otis, haven't you ever seen a pugenstein?"

Otis shook his head no.

But the pugenstein wouldn't move. He knew his job, and he wasn't going to be easily enticed by a few beginners.

"Alex, it can't hear you," Edwald reminded him, "the silence potion." Alex had already forgotten.

Edwald reached into his pocket and pulled out a biscuit.

"I keep forgetting no one can hear us." Alex wondered why they could still hear each other though. Maybe because they drank the potion together? That seemed logical. He watched as Edwald tried to entice the bulgy-eyed guardian. "How did you know to bring that cookie?"

"Pennybrown told me about him. He said he saw him peaking out of the door when he was going to Mr. Boomer's class. I figured I would come prepared."

"Smart."

Edwald threw the biscuit to the floor.

The pugenstein growled and took a cautionary step forward. After sniffing it a few times, the creature peered up with a hearty dissatisfaction.

"He doesn't like it," Edwald said, surprised.

Suddenly a jolt of electricity **zapped** from one bolt (on the pugenstein's head) to the other. It was a powerful surge, which sent the entire body off the floor. Once back down, the monster circled maniacally.

"What's it doing?" Otis asked.

"I think . . . it's looking for the electricity," Alex said.

The pugenstein gave up circling, and stopped.

"He doesn't like it," Edwald repeated again, still stupefied. "He doesn't like the treat."

The pugenstein, as though understanding the conversation, tipped his head from side to side, and looked from one boy to the other.

Edwald stomped his foot on the ground. "Books about animals are never right."

The pugenstein took one last look, and cantered back to the adjoining room.

Edwald picked up the biscuit. "I wonder what kind of treats they do like?" He promised himself to look into the mystery.

Alex had moved to the end of the chamber. There, on the floor, was a circular door. "Over here!"

Edwald ran to him. "Alex! It's a secret door! We have to open it."

Alex leaned down, grabbed the handle, and pulled. Nothing. "It won't open."

Edwald tried too, but the door wouldn't budge. "It's too heavy. Little hobgob buggers."

"Maybe they all open the door together," Alex suggested, "in alliance."

Otis stepped forward. "I'll do it," he said. His voice, unexpectedly, had become strong—powerful. Alex noticed this and thought it strange. One moment these gargoyles were shy, the next minute forceful. You couldn't pin them down.

"Great," Edwald said, and stepped back.

Otis reached down and opened the trapdor with one easy pull.

"Don't throw it," Edwald said hurriedly. "Just set it on the floor."

Otis obeyed Edwald's direction.

Suddenly the pugenstein popped his head out of the doorframe, and glared.

"Good," Edwald said. "That's done. At least it's open."

Alex poked Edwald. "He's watching us."

Edwald about faced.

The pugenstein watched them as if at attention.

"What if he barks?" Alex asked.

The pugenstein tipped its head one more time, deemed the situation unthreatening, and exited with a huff.

"All right. Let's go. I brought a torch." Edwald pulled a gnarled stick from his belt and swirled it three times. The tip ignited into flame with a quick burst. "They sell these in the store next to the weeds."

The boys peered down to the large black hole at their feet. A staircase went straight down from the circular opening into a pitch black pit. Large enough to accommodate a small hobgoblin for sure, but anyone else had to duck their head.

"Are you sure this is safe?" Otis asked.

"I don't know. I hope so." Edwald's voice was not at all reassuring.

"We can't stop now," Alex told them. "We have to keep going."

The aperture seemed menacing and sinister, with a faint musty smell rising up from the depth.

Suddenly, the pugenstein emerged in a gallop. With feet propelling (and a massive grin), the creature dashed past them and into the dark cavity.

"Wait Puggy! Wait!" Edwald yelled.

Alex felt a rush of excitement. The pugenstein knew! This was it! The Night Gallery! The first clue!

"Follow the pugenstein!" Alex yelled out, and ran down the steps in a burst of excitement.

"Wait!" Otis said. His feet were larger and the steps more difficult. "I can't go that fast!"

"Fly!" Alex said.

"I can't fly yet!" Which was true. Otis was far too young to fly.

"Follow the pugenstein!" Alex hollered out again. It was time to storm the castle. Siege the battlement! Win the prize! And they could scream as loud as they wanted! And why!? Because no one could hear them!!

"Berry-cool!" Otis caterwauled.

By the time they reached the bottom of the steps, the pugenstein was waiting, quite patiently, on the floor.

Otis fell in love with the monster in that moment. Especially the large tongue that hung out the side of its mouth.

Edward lifted up his torch to get a better view. "This is it," he said, with an excited exhale, "the Night Gallery."

22

THE NIGHT GALLERY

You may wonder, since the Night Gallery was so famous, why the older students didn't know about it. Well, actually, they did. The magical hall and the ancient paintings were legendary. But, for fear of being penalized, they never let on. Besides, they had their own riddles to solve.

The hallway was long, with a tattered red runner stretching between adjacent walls of hanging portraits. Ancient faces peered from the paintings and not all of them were friendly.

"The Vampedia was right," Alex said excitedly. "It's the ancient vampire hall."

"I didn't bring a copy of the riddle. We should have brought a copy," Otis whined. It would be impossible to go back to the wing and retrieve it now. Impossible.

"I have it." Alex hunted through his pockets.

The pugenstein watched them from the ground with perked up interest.

"It looks like it wants something."

Edwald followed Otis's gaze to the creature. "Pet him."

Otis was puzzled. "What's that?"

"Take your claw and scratch the top of his head," Edwald responded.

Otis patted the pugenstein between it's metal posts.

Edwald interjected, "Not there. You'll get zapped."

Otis yanked his hand away.

The pugenstein stared up, questioningly.

With a bit of hesitation, Otis moved his hand to the creature's backside instead and scratched. Of course, the pugenstein was very pleased with this and henceforth followed Otis throughout the room.

Where was it? Pencil, eraser, a stick of sweet candy, wallet—it was in there— somewhere. He always carried it with him.

"How much stuff do you have in your pockets?" Edwald asked, impatiently. "You're as bad as the librarian."

"Here it is." Alex finally withdrew the crinkled paper.

"Read it again," Edwald said.

Alex nodded.

"Just the first part."

"In the night gallery of the voivode, a clever woman sits. Beside her might be the key to all, but if not, then why not quit?"

Otis bit the nail of his thumb before saying, "Maybe

there's a book beside her. Or maybe she's holding one."

Surprised, Edwald exclaimed, "That's a good idea! Let's look for that."

And they did.

Alex only made it half way down the hall though before jerking to stop. Someone he recognized was in one of the portraits! A short, serious man with a strange monocle in one of his hands. The engraving read: *Duncanus Vambarey. 1034.*

Otis ran up to him. "I found her," he said, his voice flushed with gargoyle excitement. "I found her. She's over there."

"I think this is my—"

Otis tugged Alex's cape, impatiently. "Come on!" After all, this was no time for relatives!

Too true, it wasn't. "Where is she?" Alex asked.

"Down there." Otis poked his finger towards the end of the hall.

"Edwald!" Alex yell-whispered.

Edwald stood about 30 feet away, and in the opposite direction.

"Edwald!"

Nothing. His body seemed rooted to the spot, and his arm, which held up the torch, looked—*suspended.*

Alex raised his voice a little higher. "Edwald!"

Again. Nothing. Zilch.

"Otis. Something's wrong."

Both of them bounded to Edwald's side.

Alex put a hand on his friend's shoulder. "Edwald?"

But Edwald didn't move. Or turn.

"Otis, he's been mesmerized."

"Like being petrified?"

"No. Mesmerized is different."

The painting, which Edwald could not take his eyes from, was of a woman. Her face was porcelain white and her hand reached out—beckoning. From the bottom of the frame, her dress spilled from the wood casing and onto the rug liner of the hall. A diamond necklace glittered from her long, thin neck.

Alex shook him. "Edwald?"

Edwald's body swayed, but did not respond.

"What do we do?" Otis asked.

Alex shook him again, but this time harder.

"Edwald?! Wake up!"

Edwald jerked. He looked to his friends, but his eyes were still milky. "What happened?"

"You were mesmerized," Alex said firmly. "But not that deeply."

"I was?" Edwald tried to get his bearings.

In Carpathia, the power of mesmerizing can do dreadful and terrible things. Horrible things. The stronger the vampire, the more powerful the talent. But for Edwald, the talent was hardly employed. He came back to the world quickly, and without any damage.

Edwald pointed to the woman in the painting. "It's her. I think . . . I think she did it."

Alex turned to the painting. Otis did too.

"I was looking into her eyes and . . ."

Alex reassured him, "You're all right now."

Edwald said, "Her *eyes* . . ."

"Come on." Alex dragged him away. "Think of something. Your home, a tree, anything. Otis found the clever woman. Think of that."

"He did?" But Edwald kept looking over his shoulder. He could still see the dress flowing onto the carpet, and the hand—reaching out for him—

The boys reached Otis's discovery, which was much farther down the hallway, and halted.

The woman in the portrait was not reading a book, as Otis had previously suggested, but sitting calmly on a chair with her hands folded in her lap. She wore a simple black dress and her head was tilted to the side. Alex noticed her hair was strangely styled and wrapped in little buns all over. Behind a pair of pink spectacles, her green eyes beamed as if to say, *Can I help you?*

"It could be her," Alex said.

Edwald answered, "Maybe, maybe not."

The boys scrutinized the painting harder.

Alex walked up to the picture to read the name. The plaque was gone. "Her name is missing. They've taken her name," he said.

"I'll bet they did it on purpose," Otis responded, "so it wouldn't be easy."

"There!" Alex said. "Look at her feet. Those are sheets of music! Besides her might be the key to all, if not then why not quit!"

He was right, of course. Three simple sheets of music

were scattered on the floor beneath her, in the portrait.

The pugenstein barked, and looked up at them.

"The pugenstein agrees," Otis said, excitedly. "He made a funny sound."

Alex looked over to his friend, "It's called a 'bark'. The humans call it the same thing too."

"Guys!" Edwald waved his hands in the air. They were soooo close. So close. "This is it. That's the clue."

Alex walked up to the painting, reached out, and touched the picture—

A POP of light exploded, like a night burst, or a firecracker, and the sheets fell to the floor.

"That's it!" Edwald cried.

Otis yelled out a *tut tut tut* (that's a gargoyle expression, by the way), as Alex and Edwald threw themselves into each other's arms, and the pugenstein circled at their feet, barking.

Alex rushed over and picked up the papers.

"Look at the lady!" Edwald yelled out, and signaled.

Upon retrieving the music, her body had changed. Her forefinger was now pointing upward and crossing her lips, telling them—like any painting would—to shh-hhhhhhhhhhhhhhh, it's a secret.

She didn't need to say it though. They would never. Ever, ever . . . ever, ever . . . tell anyone in a million years.

"Thank you," Alex exhaled.

But the clever woman did not move, or speak, and her forefinger remained poised over her lips.

"Come on," Edwald said breathlessly. "The torch is going out."

"We did it!" Otis blurted.

"Wait 'til we tell everyone," Alex said. "They won't believe it."

And the boys swivelled around to return to their wing.

A voice halted them in their tracks. "Hi guys. What have you got there?"

"You!" Edwald exclaimed.

"Who else?"

Otis stood in awe. It wasn't possible, was it? Had a girl really crawled on her hands and knees, in the dirt, by herself, and followed them down there? Alone?

She said, "You should have invited me with you though. You would have got down here a lot faster."

Wow, Otis thought to himself. Maybe his brother was right. Maybe girls *were* smarter than boys.

23

HADRIAN'S FIRE

It was Angelica who found them in the Night Gallery. She stood before them, very much pleased with herself, and grinned. "Music. That's a good clue," she said. "Do any of you play?"

The pugenstein panted.

"*We* figured out the clue," Otis babbled.

"I know. I never said you didn't."

Alex looked at her. "How did you follow us?"

"I was coming back from the bathroom and I saw him jumping up and down." By 'him', she meant Otis.

"Oh great," Edwald said. His shoulders sank.

Angelica advanced towards Alex to examine the sheets of music.

Edwald blocked her. "I don't think so," he said.

"You may as well," she said. "Firstly, we're friends. Secondly, I haven't seen any of you in music class, have I?"

Alex felt like kicking himself for never expressing any interest in music.

"What does that mean?" Otis asked.

Angelica stared at them exultantly. "I *know* that none of you play instruments. So if none of you play, what are you going to do with the music? Have you thought about that?"

Edwald glanced to Alex.

She took another step. "That is why the end of the first part of the riddle says, then why not quit? Not just *anyone* can play a musical instrument."

Angelica turned away from them and moved to the clever lady. She touched the sheets of music in the painting, for they had reappeared, and watched them as they drifted to the ground. She quickly scooped them up. After sorting the pages carefully, she said, "Do you even know what instrument the music's written for?"

They didn't.

An evil thought flashed into Alex's mind. Later that night he would sneak into her wing and dye her hair purple. Or maybe even canary. That would get her.

She resumed, haughtily, "I didn't think so. Well, since you were so nice to lead me here, and since you are *you* Alex," she said, "I'll tell you. It's for the piano. Well, maybe harpsichord—"

Angelica's voice was cut off. A loud *BOOM!* jolted the corridor.

In an instant, everyone was thrown to the ground.

Angelica screamed.

Edwald shouted, "What's going on?!"

"I don't know!" yelled Alex.

But the impact was not a singular event, which ended after it hit, but the beginning. With every second, the quake increased.

Alex looked up and down the corridor. He could see the portraits rattling against the walls.

"The shaking! It's not stopping!" Otis bawled.

A commotion was breaking out above them.

Upstairs, in the rectangular room of jars, the glass containers were rattling and clanking, smacking against each other.

A hobgoblin's voice broke through the chaos: "The dirt! Save the dirt!"

"What do we do?!" Angelica shrilled.

As if hearing her, a hobgoblin answered with a shriek: "Save the dirt!"

Alex heard a jar fall and shatter against the floor.

A cry punctuated the air.

The pugenstein barked, in terror, as another hobgoblin wailed.

"The jars," Alex said frantically. He pulled Angelica up from the floor. "They're trying to save the jars."

"It's slowing down," Otis said. The rocking, swaying, turning, twisting, booming had subsided to a low tremor.

"Up the stairs," Edwald exhaled, as he jumped to his feet, "hurry."

The beginners dashed back down the corridor and

towards the staircase.

"They're closing the door!" Edwald yelled.

Alex could see the hobgob bodies pushing in union. The round metal top was sliding into place.

"Stop!" Alex yelled. "We're down here!"

Angelica screeched, "STOP!"

Otis ran faster—"Wait!"

Edwald yelled at the top of his lungs, "DON'T CLOSE IT!"

But the circular trapdoor continued to slide, with the sound of metal cutting against stone, and just as it was about to shut, the pugenstein dashed up the stairs, and vanished through the opening.

It sealed with a *clunk*.

"Oh no," Angelica uttered, "we're trapped."

The torch sputtered.

"The light! Don't let it go out!"

"Angelica, it's all right," Edwald consoled. He had no idea how to calm a freaked-out elemental.

Alex wondered how they were going to open the lid above them. From the staircase, it was impossible to get any leverage.

"We'll protect you," Otis insisted, "don't you worry."

Angelica looked to him, surprised. "You will?"

"Sure we will," Edwald agreed. His pride had kicked in too.

Alex tried to use his vampire vision again, but nothing happened.

Angelica spun around. "What's that?"

"What?" Edwald asked.

"I heard something."

All of them froze.

"Are you sure?" Alex asked.

"Yes," Angelica hissed, in a desperate whisper.

Suddenly, the torch fizzed, like a little firecracker, and went out.

"The beginners are the concern," the Magus said. He walked fast. Mr. Ticora marched beside him. "They are too young to know what is happening."

Mr. Ticora concurred. "I understand."

The Magus stopped. "And I don't want them to know," he said. Their eyes met. "Manton, clarify that as my bidding to the others."

Mr. Ticora's blonde mane was tousled about his shoulders and his cloak was askew. He should have been all sleepy and disoriented, but he wasn't. "I will tell them. Hadrian is already in the courtyard."

"What is happening!" It was Mrs. Philpotts. She scrambled towards them with her hands holding up the front of her nightgown.

"Mrs. Philpotts," the Magus barked. "Calm down. I don't want the children to see you looking like . . . a frazzled chicken. Help Mr. Ticora usher the students into the main courtyard. And expecially the loiterers."

She pulled herself together. "Yes, yes. Of course."

"I will attend to the Masters," he directed. "Do not allow anyone—with no exceptions—to return to their wings."

All the students, from beginners to masters, gathered in the castle courtyard. There they huddled, mostly in robes and night clothes, as Magus Whitlock swept past them and to the stone platform. The teachers were already there and standing next to their seats.

The vampire Hadrian stood in front of the quad's stage like a sentinel. He held a spear in his right hand and wore a silver bespeckled mask.

The questions ricocheted among the students like a darting faery:

"What happened?"

"What's going on?"

"Are we being attacked?"

"Is the school is being eaten up by the ground?"

And many more to that effect.

The Magus clapped his hands together, which was Hadrian's cue.

Hadrian took it and stepped forward. He tossed his spear from one hand to the other and smacked the bottom of it against the ground.

The moment the spear made contact, a blast of lightning bulleted out of the sky, sliced through the air, and struck the tip of the lancet. It stayed there like a current to the Gods and lit up Hadrian's mask-covered face.

The students gave a collective gasp.

"Do we have your attention now?" The Magus asked.

The librarian, Mrs. Moon, rushed onto the stage.

The Magus tipped his head to her as she whispered into his ear.

Batcakes, who was standing in front, could make out some of the hushed conversation. He didn't know it, but he had the rare gift of vampire hearing. In later years, he would learn how to use it.

"—trapped. Four of them. To be exact."

"And the dirt?"

"The janitors are cleaning it up. But there has been casualties. With the glass."

"Thank you Mrs. Moon."

Batcakes did not impart what he had heard. After all, why should he? To him, everyone had heard the conversation. And, since there had been no reaction, he figured the information for a bore.

The Magus turned back to the student body and raised his right hand in the air. "There is no need for upset," he said, with an emphasis on 'there'. "The castle has merely *shifted*. An unwanted surprise no doubt, but inevitable for the history of our school. Please return to your wings. Tomorrow, due to this unwanted interruption, school will commence one hour later. Now *please*. Proceed with dignity. And do not wander!"

If the Carpathian Academy ever had a screaming contest, Angelica would have won first place. The moment the darkness had taken hold, her mouth opened and she blasted everyone with another ear-piercer.

"Listen, do you want us to leave you here?!" Edwald spouted.

The threat worked, for her mouth slammed shut.

"Thank you," he said. "Now. Alex. Can you see anything?"

"Yeah. But it's not vampire vision."

"What is it?"

"I don't know, but I can see the frames glowing."

"What? From the pictures?"

"Yeah, they're glowing."

"They're not glowing to me," Angelica said. "Am I allowed to speak now?" This was directed to Edwald.

"Yes! As long as you don't scream."

"I wanted the hobgoblins to hear us, that's all."

Edwald rolled his eyes. "Yeah right."

Angelica stomped her foot. "I did!"

"You're screaming because you're a girl."

Now she was mad. "I was not!"

Alex piped in, "Who cares. It's not helping. Otis?"

"Yeah?" His voice came from the floor.

"What are you doing?"

"I'm looking for the stick," he said.

"What stick?"

"The one Edwald had. He threw it down."

"What are you doing that for?" Edwald demanded. "We have to get out of here. Who cares about a stick."

"Found it," he said.

Everyone heard a snap as Otis broke Edwald's torch in two.

"Forget the stick!" Edwald spouted in frustration. "We better start thinking. Fast. Who knows what's creeping around down here."

Otis ignored him and rubbed the two pieces together. One of the sticks ignited into flame. "Here we go," he said. Everyone could see his gargoyle smile in the light. "A torch."

Angelica clapped in delight.

Edwald was impressed. "I take back everything I said."

Alex felt a wave of pride. "Great. But let's get out of here before it goes out."

Edwald nodded. "Good idea."

"I can make it last," Otis replied, confidently. "I'm a gargoyle. Plus we have an extra." And he held up the other piece of stick.

Alex had always wondered about the Night Gallery. It was reputed to be filled with magic, weird monsters, and never ending tunnels. Like a labyrinth that never ended, or a maze of false exits. Everyone knew it was more than just a museum of paintings, but many of the corridors hadn't been explored in years, and it was told—at least in rumors—that unknown races of creatures lived there.

"Maybe we should try the lid?" Angelica asked, timidly. "Maybe we can open it."

Otis answered her. "I did that when it was dark. They locked it."

"I think we should go to the end of the hall and see where it takes us," Edwald suggested, "maybe we can get out that way."

Everyone agreed; and, since Otis was the gargoyle with fire, he was the one to lead them—down the darkened corridor of the Night Gallery, and into the maze of shadows.

24

THE PIANO ROOM

The shadows in the Night Gallery seemed to leap and dance around them. The old rug with its patterns of bulging shapes and upside-down flowers continued on and on and on.

Otis held up the torch.

Slowly, the group walked among the ancient vampire faces. The paintings not only depicted queens and kings, but all sorts of oddball characters. Soon, the hallway split into two—a corridor to the left and one to the right.

They stopped.

Angelica broke their silence. "Do you hear that?"

"You're hearing things again," Edwald said, derisively, but there was a tinge of fear in his voice. He kept looking over his shoulder. The faces of these adult vampires were scary.

Alex listened. She was right, there was something.

Some sort of sound . . .

Otis sniffed at the air. "It's music," he said. "I can smell it."

"How can you smell music?" Angelica said. She did not like the idea of music having a smell.

"I just can, that's all."

"You can't smell music. It's impossible. Music has no smell."

Otis defended himself. "It does have a smell."

"No it doesn't."

Edwald cut in, "Would you two stop fighting."

"Otis is right," Alex said. "It is music. It's coming from over there. Come on!"

All of them dashed into the left passage and rounded another corner into an adjoining hallway. In the distance, a door hung open, with light spilling out from its interior.

"It's part of the riddle," Edwald said, his voice re-energized.

As they got closer, Alex heard the soft tinkling of piano notes, swelling up like a wave of emotion, and falling back down into melancholy.

They stopped within a short distance from the door.

"Wait." Alex held up his hand. "We don't know what's in there."

"Yeah," Otis agreed. "It could be a monster."

"Let's go back. Maybe we can try the door again." Angelica was staring at the walls around them. They seemed heavier now, and spookier. The skin was starting to prickle up on her arms. "Guys, look at the portraits."

They had been doing so much running, turning, and twisting, they hadn't noticed the change of decor.

The paintings were different now. Way different. With the faces twisted into hateful expressions.

Alex stopped and looked at the closest one.

A woman looked back at him, her hair in a tight black bun, her mouth an angry line, and her moldy dress spilling out from the bottom of the frame. She looked like someone that might stomp on a dying bird. And enjoy it. Alex took note of her name. *Olga Hexler.*

"I have a bad feeling," Edwald whispered. He was using his druid sense.

"You're right." It was Otis. "This place smells like . . ." But he didn't finish his thought. Maybe it was best *not* to tell them what it smelled like.

Alex felt a wave of energy. A surge. Something shot into in his mind. "I know this place. I do!"

"Good. Where are we and how do we get out?" Edwald threw back.

"We're in a . . ." Alex gave another hesitant glance to the paintings. Was it his imagination, or did they seem to be closing in on them? "It's a . . ."

Edwald threw his arms up. "What! What is it?"

Alex finally said it. "A jail."

"What!" Angelica shrilled.

Edwald quieted her with, "Shhsssshhh," and turned to Alex. "What do you mean *jail*?"

"It's a prison for darkling vampires. The Vampire Counsel jails them in the paintings if they've done something illegal."

Otis smacked his claws to his head. "Bad, bad, bad. This is really, really bad."

"That's what I've read anyway." Alex looked at his friends. "But it can't be, right? How could that part of the Night Gallery be underneath the school?"

"Maybe we're not in the school anymore," Otis said. "Maybe it's just a portal. Like the trees we went through to get to the boats."

"What do we do!?" Angelica said frantically. "Who *cares* how we got here. How do we get out?"

"No," Edwald said. His voice was firm. "This *must* be the rest of the riddle."

"But what if it's not," Angelica begged.

"Well, we have to find out," Edwald answered.

Alex tried to think of their options. "We can't go back anyway. The janitors shut the door."

"We should go back and scream louder," Angelica offered. "We weren't loud enough."

"You certainly were," Edwald said.

Alex watched as Angelica detonated. "You! . . . you . . . druid!"

Edwald laughed. "Sticks and stones may break my bones, but telling me what I already know isn't going to hurt me."

"I hate you. You know that?"

"No you don't. You're just mad."

Otis stepped into the conversation. "Both of you stop. Alex is right. We can't go back." He paused and then went on, "We have to go into that room. Into the light."

"What if it's a ghost," Angelica told them, "it could be a ghost."

Edwald turned to her hotly. "Are you afraid of ghosts now?"

When it came to ghosts, yes, Angelica was afraid. "No," she replied, lying. "But I'd rather not meet one in *here*. And, just so you know Edwald Trowbridge, I am not speaking to you anymore!"

"Guys," Alex said nervously. "We have to hurry. The paintings . . . they're darklings."

Edwald turned on his heels and faced Alex. "All right. What is a darkling? I don't even know what that is."

Alex answered, "They're bad vampires." He pointed at one of the paintings. "See their faces? The faces reflect what they're like inside. In their hearts. Scary and meannnnn."

Suddenly Otis yelled and pointed into the darkness. "Look!"

Eyes torpedoed.

A billow of mist curled down the corridor and circled towards them like a mini tornado.

Angelica grabbed Otis's arm. "Oh no."

Down the corridor, where the light from Otis's torch faded into darkness, a figure stepped out of a painting, and into the corridor. First its foot on the rug, then the body, and finally the cape, which slid out of the interior of the frame like a snake, and swirled over the carpet. Two red eyes glimmered in the half-light.

"It's an illusion, right Alex?" Otis's gargoyle voice was riddled with fear. "Right? Just an illusion—"

"No Otis." Alex watched as a hand moved out of the mist. The fingers unfurled. "It's not."

Otis shook his gargoyle head. "Oh bats are we in trouble."

"Children," the vampire said. One foot moved in front of the other, gently. Alex could see the dark boots on the red carpet. "Come and speak with me. There's nothing to fear."

Which, of course, they all knew was a big fat lie.

Otis groaned.

Angelica screamed.

And the mist swirled up, and twisted towards them as the vampire approached.

There was nothing left to do. Now they *had* to go into the room. No matter what was in there, or who . . .

"RUN!" Alex yelled.

And they did—down the hallway, away from the darkness—and into the light.

"Does it lock? Does it lock?!" Edwald yelled, frantically.

The group had dashed into the room and thrown themselves against the door.

Alex saw the lock above the knob. He grabbed it and rammed the bolt into place.

"That was close," Otis said.

"Alex, who was that?" Edwald asked. His body pressed against the rotted wood just below the bolt.

"He can probably get through this," Alex told them. "An old door isn't going to stop a darkling."

None of them had even noticed Angelica, who now stood shaking just a few feet away. One of her fingers pointed forward, her mouth stood open quivering, and her lips jostled.

"He won't come in," a voice said, from the other side of the room.

The boys did a 360. They had been so intent on the door they hadn't even looked behind them!

Alex immediately saw a vast oval room. In the middle of it sat a vampire, cross-legged, with a huge grand piano behind him. His hands sat loosely on his uppermost knee. His red cape, which glittered from some unknown material, covered the entire expanse of the floor, and stopped just short of their feet. It was a royal cape, usually worn for special occasions, and looked like an intricate tapestry. Behind him, a candelabra sat, just past the piano, with at least a 100 candles from its many twisting stems. Alex had never seen one so big before.

The features of this vampire were odd, and all the boys noticed it immediately. The skin was too smooth, the eyebrows too high, and the lips too full. Alex thought he looked like an actor in one of the vampire picture shows. Or one of the men in his mother's magazines. Too perfect, and not quite real.

The vampire stared directly at them from his stool.

"I am Stronheim," he said.

Alex, being the only vampire in the group, stepped forward. "I'm Alex."

Angelica cut in, fearfully. She finally managed to find her voice. "Are you a . . . a . . . darkling?"

He bowed his head. "I am. Thank you."

Angelica moaned.

Alex ignored her and asked, "Are you sure he can't get in?"

Stronheim smiled. "He cannot, I assure you."

Alex advanced a few more steps. But not too many! Just in case. "Why are you . . . in here? Is this where you live?"

Stronheim did not answer at first, but instead swiveled on his stool to face his piano again. He placed his hands on the keys. "Yes Alex. This is where all of us live."

Alex reached the edge of Stronheim's cloak. From where he stood he could see a copious amount of jewels sewn into the lining.

Stronheim began to play. "We live in the pictures you see."

Alex froze.

The music floated up, like incense. Alex noticed that the song was beautiful, but sad.

"What is that you're playing?"

"This? It's a composition of my own creation. Do you like it?"

"Yes."

"It's a lonely story. It's about a boy who discovers he is not who he thinks he is."

Alex thought about the statement before answering. "Sometimes I think . . ." Alex looked back to his friends, briefly, "That . . . it's everyone's story."

"Oh yes. You are right about that." He paused before saying, "Alex Vambarey of Hillock Green." Stronheim reflected, and smiled as he glanced over his shoulder. His fingers were brushing the keys like feathers. "I have waited years to hear that name. And now you are here by chance. Isn't the world a funny place?"

Alex wondered. "I don't know. I think so."

Stronheim continued to play, the composition filling the room with wistful harmonies.

Abruptly, a voice broke the silence—"Stronheim. You've never played more beautifully."

Alex whipped around.

It was the Magus!

"Thank you David."

Principal Whitlock stepped forward. He had materialized out of thin air. "I see you've met Alex."

Stronheim crossed one hand over the other and struck a single key. He did not turn around. "We were having a lovely conversation. I was just about to dedicate this new piece to him. But, of course, it must have a telling name. Something to mark the occasion. As you know, the Atlanticans—"

"I am well aware of that Stronheim."

There was a stifled pause.

"But what to call it?" Stronheim pondered. His fingers tickled the piano. "Perhaps, '*It Has Begun*'. What do you think? An appropriate title?"

"I think peremptory," was the answer.

Stronheim stopped. He turned to Whitlock and nodded. "I quite agree," he said. "Time the devourer has no need for anyone tonight."

The Magus nodded. "Thank you Stronheim. It certainly has no need of these beginners."

"You're right David. You're so right. Forgive me."

Alex stepped forward, crossed the rest of the expanse, and offered Stronheim his hand. "It was nice to meet you Mr. Stronheim."

Stronheim's eyes widened, but relaxed quickly. Slowly, he reached his hand through the air, and took Alex's. He clasped it firmly. "Yes Alex. Until next time. When the world might need us." He paused, and opened both of his hands to everyone in the room. "When the world might need *all of us*."

VAMPIRE VALLEY

BOOK 2

OF

CARPATHIA

THE PRINCIPAL'S OFFICE

"*Commendable* beginners," Principal David Whitlock mused. He sat in his chair behind an ornate and rather enormous desk, with the chair-back twisting up behind him. It looked like the shape of carved hands and all the palms faced outward. Alex wondered if it had some magical importance. "The first part of the riddle is solved I see."

Angelica threw her hand up.

"Yes my dear."

"I thought we were supposed to give the music *to* him?" She held up the sheets. "I thought he would play it for us."

"No. The music you hold was for a beginner to play, not Stronheim." He entwined his fingers. "As you probably know, you were not meant to be in that part of the Night Gallery."

"Because of the darklings?" Alex asked.

"The school shifted just after you found the clever woman. Because of the earth ripple, the darkling section of the gallery opened, thereby admitting you. An unexpected side effect."

So that was why! Alex thought. He knew it had to have been an accident. There was no way they would have been allowed to go into that part of the museum alone. "It's a jail, right? For the darkling vampires."

"Jail?" The Magus looked at him, surprised. "No Alex. Not exactly."

Edwald spoke up. "Are there druids in there too?"

"Oh yes. The world isn't just filled with vampires Edwald." Whitlock smiled. "The gallery has every manner of creature in it. But, since there are mostly druids and vampires in our world, the other races have smaller sections." He looked at Otis when he said this. "But the others are still represented. With equal importance."

A few days later, Alex bought the *Night Gallery Compendium* from the school store. The museum was far too large to see everything, not to mention the forbidden sections, so the book helped. There, in the glossy pages you could view all the portraits, along with their descriptions. Alex's favorite was the incandescent Little Loo, pixie extraordinaire, who had saved the Minoan butterfly from extinction.

"Gargoyles too?" Otis asked.

"Without question gargoyles Otis," Whitlock answered.

"The vampire that came out of painting," Alex said, "he wanted to talk to us. That's when we ran into the piano room."

"Yes," replied the Magus, regretfully. "He did. In that section of the gallery, the vampires are confined to their paintings. But—they take turns in the piano room. As you were walking down the hall, Stronheim's time was up and Blacmar was next in the queue."

"Blacmar," Edwald said. "Is that his name?"

Whitlock nodded. "Yes. He can be . . . intimidating."

"But why did he want to talk to *us*?" Alex asked.

"It's very lonely in the Night Gallery." The Magus placed his hands flat on the desk and smiled as if thinking of a private joke. "Which means visitors are a treasured commodity."

Alex wasn't sure if the Magus was telling them everything. He had a feeling there was A LOT that he was leaving out.

"What about the woman by the stairs?" Edwald asked. "The woman in white. Is she . . . ?"

The recognition was instant on Principal Whitlock's face. He looked at Edwald directly. "Queen Margaret?"

Edwald nodded. His eyes glazed over as he remembered her dress spilling out of the frame, and the long white hand that had reached out to him.

"She is not a darkling Edwald."

"That's good," he breathed out, in relief, "Alex said she mesmerized me."

Alex watched as Whitlock scanned Edwald's face. He

was looking at him so intensely! But why?

"Most definitely not a darkling," the Magus assured, "so you had nothing to fear. Nothing at all." He clapped his hands together. "You have all had an adventurous night. Now what I suggest—"

Suddenly, the door flew open and whacked against the wall.

Two gargoyles exploded into the room, followed by a bumbling Mrs. Philpotts. Alex thought she looked like a rhinoceros in high heels, which made it really hard not to laugh. "Please! Please!" Her hands were fluttering a mile a minute.

The gargoyles, who happened to be Otis's parents, ignored Mrs. Philpotts entirely.

"Mr. Whitlock," one of them began. It was Otis's father. "We must talk!"

Otis's mother, Dee, rushed over to him protectively, and snatched him.

"I see that by sending my son to school he is already been placed in grave danger," Otis's father bellowed. His voice was so deep it resounded through the room.

Mr. Whitlock stood up from behind his desk.

"And that," Otis's father added, "is not what I call a safe education."

Dee rubbed the few strands of Otis's hair away from his forehead.

Whitlock answered very softly. "The children were *at no point* in harm's way."

Alex watched Otis's father, whose name was Tor. This

gargoyle looked absolutely nothing like the incredible masters student Lallar. Instead, Otis's father was stout and thick, muscular—all gargoyles were—and much, much older. His pointy beard looked sharp, and he had the same volcano like circles all over his skin like Otis.

"No?" Otis's father asked, haughtily. "I am thinking of withdrawing him from his courses."

At this, Otis jerked away from his mother and shouted, "Nothing happened! We only went down one hall!"

"That's all it takes," his mother snapped. Her voice rang out in the air. "One wrong hallway!"

"We were fine!" Otis retorted.

Tor did not look at his son, but put his hand out. Clearly this meant silence.

Otis shrunk back.

Whitlock slowly rose from his chair and moved to the edge of his desk. He leaned against it. "As I said, I can assure you they were in no danger. From the vampires, the paintings, or anything else."

"Assurance is not good enough," Tor said.

"I see. But perhaps you mean *my* word is not good enough. So—would you be more confident if I told you Lorcan was protecting them?"

"Lorcan!"

Whitlock nodded.

Dee's face popped with surprise.

"If Lorcan is here, I must speak with him."

"Lorcan has asked to remain removed. By special arrangement, and under certain circumstances, he has offered his aid to the school. Unfortunately I can tell you no more than that."

Tor crossed his arms. "Is this the truth?"

"Tor!" It was Dee. The question was a direct challenge. Her husband had gone too far.

Whitlock did not move from the edge of his desk. His eyes grew darker and his face stiffened. "Are you questioning Lorcan's assistance, or that the children were in no danger?"

The answer was quick. "Neither. I withdraw the question."

Dee was disturbed. She grabbed Otis again and squeezed him like a stuffed animal.

Edwald and Angelica sat in their chairs. At first the scene was quite frightening. To them, gargoyles just looked like big monsters. But once the conversation got going, neither could hide their elation. It was fun watching adults fight and get all batty.

Tor's face clouded over. "I think . . . No. I know. You would have prevented anything serious from happening." His entire body seemed to relax. His face grew kinder. "I am sure of it."

"Thank you," Whitlock said, and bowed his head.

Tor walked over to Otis and Dee. He looked down to his son. "Son. We leave you."

Dee went and took her husband's hand.

"And to all of you congratulations. On finding the first clue. Otis. Don't forget to keep your voice . . . at a good volume." Which was very good advice.

"Sure dad," Otis replied, but his voice was dejected.

Dee kissed her son on the head.

"Thank you," Tor said to the Magus. "For an apology excepted." And with that, Tor and Dee left the room.

Principal Whitlock turned to Edwald, Angelica and Otis. "All right. The show is over. Now, off to bed. All three of you. Except you Alex. I would like you to stay for a moment."

Angelica, Otis, and Edwald went back to their wings while Alex stayed behind.

"Alex, I want you to forget what Stronheim told you. He likes to stir up trouble."

"But—"

"No Alex." Whitlock went back to the other side of his desk and sat down. "Just forget what he said. All right?"

Alex stared at the strange hands that reached up and stretched out from the chair behind Principal Whitlock's head.

"He said he'd been waiting years to hear my name. Why?"

The Magus remained silent.

"Please, I need to know."

Principal Whitlock nodded. "And you have every right to know. Your destiny is locked up with Stronheim. How exactly, is uncertain."

"Just like Pelagia," Alex mumbled.

"Pelagia?"

Alex looked up. "An Atlantican girl swam up to us

in Olaf's boat. She gave me this necklace." He held it up. The silver chain glimmered in the light.

"Interesting. Very interesting."

"I think they're connected," Alex said.

The Magus bent his head. "They are Alex. They are connected. But—do you really want to know what will happen to you in the future?"

"I think so."

"And if you knew the future, what would you do? Change it?"

Alex didn't know what to say. "I'm not sure."

"No. You would not," Whitlock said, solidly. "Enjoy what is right in front of you. What is happening *right now*. That is what is important."

Alex was disappointed. He tried to hide it, but couldn't.

"Well, I suppose I can tell you a little something. You are destined for—" and he chose his words carefully, "an *adventure*."

"I am?"

"Oh yes. A great one. You, and your friends. And I am not speaking of the riddle Alex. I am speaking of something far greater. A journey, you could say." The Magus leaned over his desk and looked directly into Alex's eyes. "Some might even say, a test."

"Test?"

"Yes. The greatest test any of us will ever take. And by *any of us*, I mean all the fine creatures of Carpathia."

"The humans . . . they are going to be involved in

this *test*, right? Somehow?"

Alex registered the surprise on the Magus's face. It was undeniable. "Yes Alex. They are."

"I had a feeling. I don't know. I just did." He paused. "I was just thinking that maybe the humans are so advanced now—I mean, we haven't seen them for so many years—that they no longer fail. What I mean to say is, they don't lose anymore. They only succeed. At everything. Maybe that's what they can do. Perhaps *that* is what humans have that we don't."

The Magus was smiling strangely. Alex couldn't place the expression. "Perhaps. But I think it is more likely that they have learned that losing doesn't matter. It's the trying that really counts."

"Well maybe they can help us then!" Alex exclaimed. "With our test. Especially if they succeed at everything. Do you think they would?"

The Magus shook his head from side to side. "Oh Alex. I hope so." His eyes glazed over as if remembering some long lost era. "I really do."